DAGON

CONDEMNED

AVA BENTON

1

DAGON

Nine Months Ago

I took the final kill shot, laughing when it struck home. That last blow led to another victory in the first-person shooter game I was playing with Zane. My roommate.

He slumped on the couch, defeated. He was tall like me but skinny as a damned rail. He had shaggy brown hair that hung to his shoulders and had numerous random tattoos he'd accumulated over the years. It was our first week back for the new fall semester. We decided to celebrate getting a larger apartment on campus with a night of gaming and beers.

"That's it, I'm not playing with you anymore," Zane muttered, tossing his controller aside.

"Oh, come on, don't be like that," I teased.

"You're reading my mind. I know you are. Such a cheater," he said, winking while he whined.

I placed my hand over my heart. "I swear I've never used my unique talents while gaming."

"Why don't I believe you?"

"I don't lie." I stood to grab us another round of beers. "Mack going to be here soon?"

"Yeah, had to stop and grab some food," Zane said.

His long-time friend Mackenzie, who went by Mack, was one of the only other friends I had on campus. The nature of being a demon was a deterrent to most humans. Zane was the exception since he was my roommate and had been for a while now. He'd been unsure of me at first but quickly got past whatever worries he had and became my friend. Mack was the same. Two friends were all I needed to get me through my days and remind me that I could pull off living amongst the humans for the rest of my life.

As long as Arkon, one of my older brothers, stopped being a damned bastard with a death wish, we might actually pull off convincing the Under-world we were dead.

Posing as a college kid had been far easier than I expected. I picked one in the small town of Wellsville, Missouri, with just a big enough population that I wouldn't stick out. Let me have a place to live, a stipend for being a TA now that I was in grad school, it gave me a great place to blend in. To disappear.

I hadn't intended to get close to anyone, not with my gift of visions which could portend positive—or terrifying—news. But after being a loner for the first couple years, it was nice having the guys around. They were both twenty-seven, the same age as me. Mack was in grad school, too. Zane was still figuring out what he wanted to do. I was reasonably sure he was going to be a perpetual student. Having them in my life meant my brothers didn't spend too much time worrying about me being on my own.

My oldest brother, Calrod, was usually too busy keeping an eye on Arkon and ensuring he didn't land his ass in a world of hurt. Neither of them visited much, and that was alright with me. We had to figure out these new lives of ours on our own. Otherwise, we'd never find a way to move past the tragedy that befell our family and simply enjoy life again.

The door to the apartment opened, and I closed the fridge, ready to greet Mack. He was stockier than Zane and me, a few inches shorter, and had short blond hair that liked to stick up at weird angles most days. He sported his typical jeans with holes in the knees, sneakers, and a vintage light green tee. He stepped inside, lifting a case of beer in one hand.

"Evening, boys," he said with an easy grin.

"Thought you were in charge of food?" I asked. "Beer doesn't count."

"I brought it; don't you worry. Should be enough pizza for the four of us."

I wondered if he'd already been drinking, considering he had no pizzas in his hands, and there were only three of us. He stepped aside, and someone else entered the apartment behind him.

"Morgan!" Zane exclaimed. "You finally got her to leave her books behind for a night? What did you bribe her with?"

"Ha, very funny, asshole," the woman, Morgan, replied with a smile that had me grinning in turn. Her eyes flitted around the apartment, giving it an appraising glance.

"You have a very long history of hiding."

"I have my reasons," she said to Zane, her smile faltering. She set the stack of pizzas on the counter, then turned and jumped, chuckling. "Oh, hey, you must be Dagon. Mack's told me all about you. I'm his little sister." She held out her hand to me.

Numbly, I took it, forcing a smile to remain on my face while my eyes danced over her. "He's mentioned you a few times," I said, recalling all the stories Mack had shared of Morgan, himself, and Zane growing up together and getting into trouble. "Nice to finally meet you."

"Likewise."

We kept shaking hands as if neither of us wanted to let go. Her dark chestnut hair was pulled back in a bright purple hair clip, with two strands of wavy locks framing her face. Her right ear was decorated with neon dinosaur studs from the lobe to the upper curve. Her lips were full and entirely kissable. I wasn't sure where that thought came from and pushed it aside. The curves of her cheeks were irresistible as well. My hand ached to trace the edge of her face down to her jaw. Her left eyebrow had a slightly higher arch to it. When she smiled again, it was like she was giving me an inquisitive look without even trying. The sleeveless purple shirt she wore flowed over her body, leading to a pair of snug-fitting ankle jeans. Two chunky bracelets adorned her wrists, one amethyst and the other moonstone. Her sneakers matched her shirt, hair clip, and earrings.

I laughed at the sight of it all.

"I amuse you already?" she said. "That wasn't hard."

"You're a very detail-oriented person, aren't you," I replied.

She shrugged, still holding my hand.

"I have my moments, I guess."

"Yeah, she is," Mack yelled from the living room.

She flipped him off. He beamed at her then turned to Zane.

Morgan's light brown eyes did a quick onceover of me, too, and she caught her tongue between her teeth, giving me an appreciative look. Her reaction confused and elated me at the same time. There was no moment of hesitation on her part, not even a little bit at being near me.

"Might need our hands to eat," she whispered.

"Huh?" I looked down and reluctantly released her. "Sorry. Got a little distracted."

"It's alright. You're not alone. So, you're in the same grad program as me, right? I saw you in a few of my classes last year."

Was she in my classes? How had I not noticed her before? "You sure?"

"Pretty sure," she said, chuckling. "To be fair, I sit in the very back. Tend to keep to myself." She shoved her hands in her back pockets, shifting on her feet. When she appeared to be holding her breath, I debated chancing a peek inside her mind but stopped at the last second. "That's strange," she whispered.

"What is?" I asked, and she jumped like she'd forgotten I was there.

"Oh, uh, nothing. I'm hungry. You boys going to eat, or do we get it all?" she asked Zane and Mack.

The guys joined us in the small kitchen, and we dished out pizza and beers. Mack hung back, clapping me on the shoulder.

"Hope you don't mind I brought her along," he told me. "She doesn't get out much."

"Any particular reason why?"

His brown eyes, dark where his sister's were light, narrowed with concern. "She's always been a bit of a bookworm. Likes to keep to herself. I'm slowly working on breaking her out of her shell. It hasn't been easy. Figured meeting someone new—like you—might be good."

"Really? You think I can help her or something?"

I mused. "Why? I don't exactly do well with the whole dating thing, if you recall."

"Maybe not, but call it a brotherly hunch," he replied.

"Are you trying to set me up with your sister?"

"She hasn't been out with anyone in years," he emphasized. "I could think of worse guys for her to date."

He walked away without giving me a chance to say anything. It was true I didn't date, and for a damned good reason. I sensed eyes on me and paused in swallowing my beer. My gaze flicked up, and there was Morgan, eyeing me curiously from the couch. She grinned, and her eyes crinkled, becoming little more than slits. I pictured myself striding across the room, holding her in my arms, and kissing her, just like that.

My hand tightened on the beer bottle, imagining that kiss leading to so much more. A possessive need to have her and get her away from the guys made me growl. I covered it up with a cough, then turned my back to the living room and those light brown eyes which were watching me. What the hell had that been about? Mack was her brother, and Zane was clearly not her type. Why did I even care if he was?

My fangs extended, threatening to shatter my

glamour. I forced my mouth to stay closed until I got them to shrink back down. There was no reason for this reaction. I glanced over my shoulder, but Morgan was engrossed in the action movie Zane had put on the TV. There was something about her I couldn't quite place. She was more than a mere bookworm. That was far too easy of an explanation for why Mack labeled her as a loner. I'd sensed it the second she walked into the apartment.

Morgan Nelson was not an ordinary human.

Not that it made any difference. No matter what Mack might hope, I couldn't allow myself to get close to anyone, not in that way. The risks were too high.

I was ready to join them in the living room, but a searing pain shot across my forehead. Cursing, I mumbled to Zane about getting a migraine and locked myself in the bedroom. Through the door, I heard Morgan ask if I was alright but I didn't get a chance to find out what Zane told her.

I gasped, sinking to my knees on the old, threadbare maroon rug in my room. My claws extended, digging through the fibers and into the hard floor beneath.

Images flooded my mind, twisting and morphing until they finally took shape.

Morgan's face appeared through the haze. She

was smiling brightly, joy lighting up her eyes. She turned, and there, by her side, was me. The air escaped my lungs at the vision of the two of us together. I drew her into my arms and kissed her. The moment was so full of love and life I couldn't hold back the smile that spread across my face while I knelt on the bedroom floor.

As quickly as the moment appeared, it darkened and became tinged in red. Blood streaking her face, Morgan was torn away from me. Pain was etched in the frown lines of her face, and she screamed. Her hand reached out. A shadow loomed upward behind her, its evil red eyes leering while it closed in on her. She curled into herself, and then the shadow consumed her.

The vision ended, and I collapsed to the floor, my stomach spasming. I lurched to my feet and made it to the trash can in time to lose the beer I'd already drunk. I'd been having visions since I was a toddler. Never had one affected me to this extent, not even after witnessing our parents' deaths. That had been horrible, but it hadn't left me shaking and covered in a cold sweat. Resting with my back to the wall, I shoved my wet hair from my face, working on getting my breathing under control.

I'd seen Morgan and me together. We'd been

happy, but then something came after her. Came after both of us? Shit, what had that thing been? It wasn't a demon. I'd never seen a shadow with such murderous eyes or felt such terror in a creature's wake. If that thing was coming after her, I had to stop it somehow. Hell, I had to figure out what it was first.

Until I did, Morgan wasn't safe.

The first part of the vision only added to my confusion. I'd never seen two possible futures at the same time. My heart sank at the next thought. I dragged my claws across the floor, creating deep rivulets in the wooden planks.

Unless—

Was destiny telling me our being together would lead to Morgan's death?

How was I supposed to make certain she wasn't killed by that monster while staying as far away from her as possible? I stared at the door, wanting to be out there by her side. Wanting to feel that same passion I'd picked up in the vision.

But I couldn't. The closer I let myself get to Morgan, the more danger she'd be in.

"Just stay away," I whispered to myself. "You can guard her from a distance. She never has to know what she's missing."

Using the wall, I hoisted myself upright, ensured my stomach was settled, and took another few seconds to wipe the last of the sweat from my brow. I ran my fingers through my hair, steeled my nerves for what I had to do, and walked out the bedroom door.

2

DAGON

Present Day

A chilly night wind blew through my hair. Tree branches creaked and groaned. They were covered in buds that had yet to fully open. Spring was slow coming this year, and the cold of winter kept threatening to return. It might be the first week of April, but it felt closer to January. Another long day of playing Morgan's silent guardian had come and gone. Like with all the others, no monstrous creature crept out of the shadows to kill her. No looming red eyes appeared to take her from me.

Not that she was mine to take. I wanted her. Gods, I hadn't stopped wanting her since the first night she shook my hand and stared into my eyes without apprehension or intimidation.

Morgan was mine, but I couldn't have her.

My steps slowed as I neared my apartment building and I glared at the sidewalk beneath my boots. For the last nine months, my main focus had been keeping an eye on Morgan and guaranteeing the vision I had never came true. But in keeping her safe, it meant the first half of the vision, the one where I saw us together, could never become a reality. I wasn't sure how much longer I could endure her worried glances or her longing stares which had caught me off guard more than a few times.

And her thoughts—

Damn what went on inside that woman's head.

If I didn't figure out a way to stop from slipping into her mind, I was going to make myself go insane. She wanted me, too, after all this time. Wanted me as severely as I craved her. If she didn't stop daydreaming about us, my entire plan to stay away would shatter.

Not that I could strictly come out and tell her why I kept my distance. She had enough issues of her own to deal with aside from learning demons were real, and I was one of them.

In all the time I'd spent observing Morgan, I had

yet to understand what she was. She shied away from large crowds as much as she could. After she told me about sitting in the back of our lecture halls, it'd been easy to find her once they'd started back in August, since we shared some of the same courses again. She sat as close to the door as possible, and away from the other students. The longer she was in a crowd, the more uncomfortable she became. I'd lost count of how many pens she'd snapped in half from twisting them.

Some days, I was worried she was going to rip her ear from how hard she tugged on her array of studs. She only hung out with her brother, Zane, or one other person. I thought her name might be Kayla. Aside from them, there was no one else in Morgan's life.

No guys, either. Seeing her out on a date with anyone other than me wouldn't have gone well.

Morgan was a mystery.

She wasn't a witch, as far as I could tell, but she was damned sensitive to whoever was around her. There were times she'd rub her back like it hurt. She'd cringe and rush to get back to her apartment like she was running from something. I'd subtly asked Mack more about her back in the beginning. He'd told me if I wanted to know about her, I should ask her. Vaguely, I circled back to the idea that she was an empath of some kind. She certainly wasn't a psychic. She would've called me out by now if she were.

"Doesn't matter what she is, remember?" I whispered to myself, continuing to walk to my apartment building. "You're only watching over her long enough to kill that shadow monster, then you're leaving her alone for good."

Being with me merely opened the avenue for her to get dragged into a deadly situation, just as Jasmine had been dragged into with Arkon. He'd suffered through her death, only to have her saved by Cyrene, a local witch. If not for Cyrene, Arkon would've lost the only woman he ever loved and probably gotten himself killed trying to avenge her.

I wanted my brothers to be happy. Fortunately, they didn't have the same gifts that I did. They never had to fear seeing someone they cared for being ripped apart and killed before their eyes. I'd hoped not getting involved with Morgan beyond being an acquaintance would've stopped the onslaught of visions. Once a week, like clockwork, I was struck with the same two flashes replaying in my mind. I'd see us together, happy and in love.

And right after, that shadowy monster would

loom up behind her and kill her while she screamed for me.

During winter break, I almost made the decision not to come back. Her fate was tied to my presence, and if I wasn't here, then the monster wouldn't go after her. That was my belief until I was bombarded with the vision every night until I chose to return to campus. Whatever was coming for Morgan wasn't going to quit. I had to stay close by so when it finally made its move, I could stop it.

These days, I wasn't merely prowling campus to keep an eye on Morgan. Five murders had occurred around Wellsville, their bodies found in the woods surrounding campus. For some reason, I was shown glimpses of each victim being hunted down and slaughtered. For the past month, I spent my nights wandering the woods in search of those who might be killing random people. So far, I'd turned up nothing but dead ends, just like the cops. They'd only found the bodies thanks to the tips I'd called in. Otherwise, it probably would've been weeks, maybe longer, before their bodies were found.

A sharp pain in my forehead made me trip over my feet just as I reached the door to my building. I fell into the brick wall, gritting my teeth and waiting for images to bombard me.

The images came. A guy around my age was running. Looked like the woods. Something was chasing him. He was panicking and yelling for help. Whatever was behind him barreled through the underbrush like a bull, but that growl was beastly. The man screamed, and the vision cut off.

I gasped, my stomach heaving. The woods. The man was in the woods. It was just like all the other visions I'd had of the murder victims, only this time I recognized the exact location. There was a dead tree not too far from campus that had a massive crack running down the center from when it'd been struck by lightning. Rumors had spread about how the tree and the dead clearing around it were haunted.

And the guy in my vision had run right past that very same tree.

The sprint to get to that part of the woods took a solid ten minutes. All the visions before had all been random glimpses of trees. It'd taken me forever to sniff out the bodies. I didn't slow my pace until I spotted the break in the trees up ahead. The night was overcast, but being a demon gave me the ability to see in the dark.

I smelled the harsh metallic tang of blood though there was no sign of a body yet. Keeping to the shadows, I shut my eyes, searching for anyone else that might be present. If they were close enough, I'd be able to get inside their heads, maybe finally figure out who this killer was.

A minute went by, then another, but no one was around me. No human. No beast. Nothing but a few owls hooting back and forth and the skittering of raccoons or possums in the bushes.

I pushed several low-hanging oak branches out of the way and stepped into the clearing where nothing grew through the charred earth. The oak tree at the center was cracked right down the middle, the bark permanently scarred from the errant bolt that struck it. Its barren branches stretched up to the night sky. By all rights, the tree should've collapsed by now, but its roots held firm.

I was a few steps into the clearing then stilled. The heavy scent of magic struck my nose, and I sneezed. Breathing in deeply, I picked up on several scents. Mandrake, sandalwood, and vervain were chief among the others too faint for me to decipher. Someone cast spells out here recently. Further examination of the clearing revealed what remained of black candles amongst the dead grass. I thought there might be a symbol laid out using some sort of white powder, possibly eggshells, but the wind had disrupted it too much for me to make out. I hadn't picked up on magic with the last five bodies. Either the killer was getting sloppy, or I'd just missed them. I moved closer to the tree, keeping my gaze focused on the ground for any more clues to give me a lead.

"Gods," I exclaimed, growling when I came around the far side of the tree and stumbled upon a grisly scene. "Just like the others."

What was left of the body was scattered in a circle, blood splattered across the ground and on the trunk of the dead tree. An arm lay a few yards off, beside what I thought were chunks of a spine. The face I'd seen in my vision stared up at the sky, his mouth frozen open in horror at being ripped apart. The wounds were jagged like something had torn through his skin with claws. I'd have to put in an anonymous call to the cops once I was finished here as I had with the others. No one else needed to stumble across this body and live with the resulting nightmares.

I was about to turn away when a glint of silver near where the torso rested caught my eye. Brushing away a chunk of flesh with muscle still attached, I picked up the length of silver chain. A small, round amulet hung from it, a circle on it with a half-circle resting atop it. A spark of violet light shot out from it.

I waited for anything else to happen. When nothing did, I clutched the necklace in my hand and straightened.

He'd been a witch.

Now a question remained. Whether the other victims were also witches or if this was merely a fluke. I hadn't found any evidence left behind in the others' remains. Grunting, I threw my head back and glowered at the sky.

I'd been putting off making a call to my brothers about the murders, but if witches were involved, it was probably time to at least talk to Cyrene. The last thing I wanted was my brothers showing up here, yet Calrod was better at tracking than me. And he had actual firepower. If someone were hunting down witches, we needed to know so we could warn them.

Calrod and Arkon could remain in the dark about what else I'd spent the last nine months doing.

I shoved the necklace deep in my pocket and jogged to campus, making a call to the cops from one of the emergency phones along the way. I rattled off what I'd seen and hung up on the guy asking me a stream of questions. Pondering over who would be crazy enough to start a feud against witches, I set off for my apartment for the second time that night. I came around a corner, head down, and walked right into someone else.

"Shit, sorry," I mumbled, catching the person's arms, then stilled. "Morgan?"

"Oh, hey Dagon." Her smile was stiff, and she was shaking.

I'd seen her go into her apartment earlier tonight. I'd made sure she was there. What the hell was she doing wandering out here alone? I growled, quickly turning it into a harsh cough at her glance.

"Why are you out here?" I demanded.

Her already arched brow went up even more. "Good night to you too." She looked to where I still held her. Reluctantly, I released my hold. It was the first time I'd touched her since we'd first met, and my hands ached to do it again.

"It's late. Not exactly safe to be out by yourself."

"Thanks for the tip," she muttered and made to step around me.

I moved, blocking her way. "Your apartment's the other way," I pointed out.

"And?"

"I'll walk you back to it."

She blinked at me twice, then burst out laughing. "Yeah, not happening. I don't need an escort."

"I'm not letting you stay out here by yourself."

"Why are you so worried about me? Not as if we're friends or anything else that matters."

My jaw clenched at the hurt in her words. We'd had one evening together, hanging out with Zanc and Mack, just one. We bumped into each other here and there with the occasional polite conversation. That was it. She shouldn't feel anything for me. I guess my pretending to be disinterested in her did the opposite of making her not care about me. It seems like it pissed her off instead, and from the way she crossed her arms and how her fingers twitched, she hadn't stopped being angry at me. No, not just angry. She was worried about me. Why?

"I'm looking out for you," I finally said.

Her brow crinkled, and those light brown eyes of hers glimmered. Her pupils dilated, and I caught a flicker of her desire springing to life. I shouldn't have done it, but I chanced a peek inside her mind. Her thoughts were a maddening swirl of unease and exhaustion. Breaking through that tempest was the same desire I'd seen in her eyes.

A flash of what was in her mind made my heart pound. She imagined our kissing. She tensed, annoyed at what she imagined doing with me, and it didn't stop with a simple kiss. The attraction I felt to her that night had only grown in both of us over the past few months.

Some days, when we brushed by each other or were stuck in the same room, the tension between us was so thick, it was like wading through a pool of water. Her thoughts continued to shift and morph until we were tangled in each other's arms, falling into her bed.

I broke the mental connection and stepped back. "Dagon?"

"I'm sorry," I whispered, hating what I'd done to her. "You really shouldn't be out at night."

"Couldn't sleep." She tugged on her heavy purple cardigan, shivering at the breeze blowing her hair around her shoulders. "Walking sometimes helps."

"How often do you do this?"

She shrugged. "A few times a week."

Was she insane? All those times, I hadn't been able to keep an eye on her. Any one of those nights could've been when the shadow monster attacked.

"What is wrong with you?" I snapped, not sure if I was more furious with her or myself. "You know about people getting slaughtered, and you think it's a great time to be out and about?"

"And like I said, why do you care, huh? No one's been murdered on campus."

"No, just in the woods around campus," I blurted. "You're being careless and stupid."

Her bitter laughter should've been enough warning to make me back down. Too bad I was no good at following those signs. "Stupid? That's what you're calling me?"

"It's the truth."

"Screw you, jackass." She shouldered past me, storming down the sidewalk. I fell in line behind her. She shot me a furious glance over her shoulder and picked up the pace, but I easily stayed with her. She came to a sudden stop and whirled around. "What is it with you?"

"I'm not going to let you stay out here by yourself."

"I'm a grown-ass woman. I think I'll be alright."

"And I say you won't be."

"So now that I might be in trouble, you'll talk to me?"

"I talk to you," I argued.

She laughed loudly.

"What?"

"You say hi to me, maybe," she corrected harshly. "You give me this weird little nod as you walk by if I'm at your apartment with Zane and Mack. Then you have the nerve to always bump into me throughout the day or check me out when you think

I'm not looking or do shit like this. You're a piece of work, you know that?"

I took another step back, but nothing aside from walking away would break the tension building between us once again. "I don't know what you're talking about."

"Bullshit. You know, I'd be okay if you'd just tell me you don't like me like that, but that's not the truth, is it? You do like me, and you're just too scared to admit it. Why?"

"Can we not do this tonight?"

"You're not going to run away from me this time," she warned. "Just talk to me. We had a connection that first night. You can't say otherwise."

"How would you know?"

She started to speak, then cut herself off, digging the toe of her shoe into the sidewalk. "I just know. Is it because you're friends with Mack or something?"

"That's not it."

"Then what?"

"You won't understand. Let it go."

"I can't. Not when you've changed so much since that night."

A nervous laugh escaped my mouth, and I rubbed the back of my neck. "I haven't changed."

"You don't smile anymore. Or laugh. You look

exhausted all the time. And I feel—" she started, stopped, and let out a heavy sigh. "I think whatever you're dealing with has to do with me, but I don't know what it is, so can you please just tell me what's going on so I can stop imagining a bunch of horrible scenarios?"

And here I thought I was the only one doing the watching. What was I supposed to do? Tell her the truth? Yeah, that'd go over really well.

"Fine, you know what, keep being a stubborn ass. Why should I care?" she said, breaking the silence. She turned around and walked past me. I should've let her keep going, but my body reacted, and I snagged her hand.

"You don't have to worry about me. You don't even know me."

"But I do. More than you realize."

"Well, you shouldn't. You shouldn't want anything to do with me."

"You think you're saving me from you or something?" She shook her head, squeezing my hand. "As far as I can tell, you're not a bad guy."

"Because you don't know everything and you can't, so just drop it. Worry about yourself. I'm walking you back to your apartment, and that's it."

I waited for her to start moving. She looked like

she was ready to hit me but shoved her hands in the pockets of her cardigan and set off. I stayed at her side, my head on a swivel, watching the grounds. Being so close to her was quickly driving me to the edge of my control. Didn't help that I'd seen what she fantasized about. I wish I could say I didn't have the same dreams, but I did. All the time. Too bad they were punctuated by nightmares of her being attacked. Her hand brushed against mine, and a surge of longing so fierce hit me hard enough to leave my knees wobbly. This was wrong. Everything about what I was doing was wrong.

The second I met Morgan, I knew she was mine. Every day without her was a waste. I wanted her to know the truth, all of it. The reckless need to come clean had my mouth opening, ready to do that. We were outside her building. She had her hand on the door, and I called her name to stop her. Her gaze landed on me, but the words never made it out.

I cursed, smashing a hand to my face.

"Dagon?" Morgan asked, squeezing my hand. "What's wrong? Is it a migraine?"

I tried to tell her I was alright, but the pain was excruciating, and I growled. My claws extended, and I tore myself away from Morgan, turning my back to her. The vision erupted into living color inside my head.

Morgan's pained shriek echoed in my ears. Her face appeared right after, eyes wide and chest streaked with blood. Three slashes marred her body. A roar seemed to come from all directions at once, closing in on her. It was dusk, and she was sprinting across a gravel drive. The ground trembled. A dark shadow loomed over her then—

Nothing. The vision ended, and I slumped over only to be caught by a set of arms.

"Come on, let's get you back to your apartment," Morgan said, supporting me.

"I'm fine," I uttered, drenched in a cold sweat and shaking.

"Yeah, sure you are."

Panic set in, and I forced myself out of her embrace. My claws and fangs, had they broken through the glamour? Had she seen the real me?

"What are you doing, you moron?" she snapped.

"Just get yourself inside." The magic holding my glamour in place slipped, and I willed it to not fail, not yet. "Promise me you won't leave your place again at night, not alone."

She pursed her lips but sighed. "I promise."

I hurried away, sensing the magic flickering in and out.

"I'll see you tomorrow," she called after me.

I growled at the promise in those words. She wasn't going to let me stay in the shadows any longer. If she found out what I was, what I was seeing, it'd complicate her life even more. And the visions, they were only going to get worse.

What the hell had I just done?

3

MORGAN

Keys jingled outside the apartment door.

I was hanging out at Zane's place with Mack tonight. I perked up, turning away from the TV, but the sound passed by. There was no telltale hint of surging energy that would announce Dagon was back. Last night had left me with more questions about who he was and why he felt the need to pretend there was no spark between us.

Or what I'd seen when he'd had his migraine attack.

I squeezed the throw pillow tighter to my chest, remembering those few strange seconds. It'd been dark, but it wasn't pitch black. Dagon's messy black hair had lightened in color around his face, turning silver and white. His nails had darkened and looked longer and curved, almost like claws. A strange pale green hue had surrounded him, but it wasn't any of those changes that left me unable to sleep.

It was the other thing I saw.

Horns.

I'd seen short, twisted horns atop his head right behind his hairline.

I wasn't exactly one to shy away from unexplainable things in this world. I was fairly certain I was a sensitive of some kind. I just hadn't figured out what to call myself. Some days I picked up on emotions. Others, it was all about energy. Every day was the same, though. It was hard to think straight and even harder sometimes to know what I was feeling.

That was until Dagon came into my life.

Something about his energy calmed the craziness, until all I picked up on was him and me. I'd wondered a few times if he was like me. After last night, my suspicion about his being different was proven correct. Now, I just had to figure out exactly what I'd seen. It wasn't probable. I believed in ghosts and shit like that, but horns? That would make him, hell, I wasn't even sure I was willing to let myself think of that possibility.

I kept expecting fear to set in. All that did change

was my concern for him shot up even higher. He'd been going through something since the night we met. He'd had a migraine that night, too. I was starting to believe his migraines weren't simply headaches.

The sound from the TV cut off. I jerked around, glancing from Zane to Mack. "What?"

"You're doing it again," Zane said, flipping the remote casually in his hand.

"Doing what?"

"Acting weird," Mack said, and my brow rose. "Weirder than normal. What's going on with you?"

"Just having a tough week. Nothing weird about that. Can we finish the movie?"

"It's Friday," Zane told me. "If he takes off like this, it means he's not coming back 'til Sunday."

"Who?"

"Who do you think? We're not blind." Zane set the remote on the table, slouching in the overstuffed black armchair. "We see how you two dance around on another. Freaking ridiculous. Any idiot can tell you two like each other. Figured by now one of you would've made a move."

"He started that shit." I pushed off the couch and stomped around the living room. My hands twined together incessantly. I'd wanted to bug Zane about

Dagon all day, but it sounded crazy in my mind, someone having horns. It would sound even worse if I said it aloud.

A throw pillow flew toward my head, and I caught it, scowling at Mack.

"Spill. Did something happen we don't know about?"

"You could say that." They scooted to the edge of their seats, eyes wide and expectant. "You're worse than the gossipers on campus. You know that?" When neither of them turned away, I lobbed the pillow at Mack and muttered, "We might've gotten into a fight last night."

"About what?" Zane asked.

"I was out for a walk, and he freaked out on me about it not being safe. Called me stupid." I planted my hands on my hips.

"Why were you out last night?" Mack asked, pushing to his feet. "After dark? Alone?"

"I do it all the time," I reminded him. "Helps me clear my head so I can sleep."

"They found another body last night." Mack marched toward me, shaking his head. "He was a student."

I crossed my arms in the face of his growing annoyance. "And?"

"And he was found by that old clearing in the woods. I think Dagon has every right to be aggravated at you for being so reckless. I am, too. Damn it, Morgan, you're supposed to talk to me when you're having trouble, not go walking around campus in the dead of night."

"You don't exactly help me anymore," I confessed, wincing at the sting of hurt coming from him.

I took a couple of steps away and shut my eyes. I had to stay focused on myself. The energy in the apartment shifted from being peaceful to tense, and I cursed, making for the door.

"Where are you going?"

"Away from you two. None of this is helping me right now," I told Mack.

"I'm sorry," he said, and I stopped at the door with my purple-flowered crossbody purse clutched in my hand. "Don't go yet. This is supposed to be our fun Friday night hang-out."

"And I'm doing a great job of ruining it." I tossed my purse back on the table by the front door and ran my fingers through my hair. They got stuck when I hit the clip. Cursing more, I yanked it out of my hair and shook out my hair until it was a tangled mess.

"Aside from Dagon getting mad at you for being

outside, what exactly did you two talk about?" Mack asked, his eyes narrowed. "Do I need to kick his ass or something?"

"What? No, why would you say that?"

"It's a big brother thing. It's what I do."

"No, you don't need to kick his ass." The possible claws and horns I'd seen on Dagon made me pretty sure my brother would lose in a brawl against Dagon anyway. "We just had a disagreement, and then he got a migraine and stormed off."

"Disagreement about what?" Zane pushed, joining us in the kitchen.

I went to the fridge and snagged three more beers, handing them out to the guys. "Stuff."

"Way to be specific." Zane popped the cap off his beer and tossed it over the breakfast bar and into the sink. "Did you two finally kiss?"

"What?" I exclaimed. "No, just no. It wasn't anything like that."

"But you want it to be," Mack chimed in, and I was ready to smack him upside the head.

"I don't know what I want. I just— He confuses me so much. One second, he's ridiculously polite, and the next, he's openly checking me out. Then last night, he went all protector mode on me. It was strange, and there's something else going on with him."

"What do you mean?" Zane asked.

"You should know. You're his roommate."

"I've been on a lot of dates lately," Zane explained with a shrug. "Haven't exactly been around to notice much. Besides, he's hardly ever here."

"How many classes is he taking?" Mack asked.

"Five last time I checked, but one of them is online, and the other is a once-a-week meet-up. I honestly have no idea where he's been." Zane tilted his beer to me. "Not gonna lie, I thought you two were dating and just not letting the rest of us know."

I wished that was the case. "He's really been gone that much?"

Zane nodded, draining half his beer. His brow furrowed, and he picked at the label. "I guess I should've asked him what was going on."

"Then you noticed how much he's changed, too?"

Zane scratched his forehead, the energy coming off him darkening. "I did, but I thought it was shit going on with his family. He told me a few years back that one of his brothers likes to get into trouble, and the oldest is always having to get him out of it."

He started to say more but went back to drinking his beer instead.

"You know something else," I accused.

"Maybe, but I'm not going to tell you. Want answers? You need to talk to him. Shit, it's like I'm a freaking broken record over here. I've been saying the same shit about you to him for months now." His eyes widened, and Mack and I shifted closer. "Can we pretend I didn't say that?"

"He's been asking about me?"

Zane sighed, hanging his head. "Off and on, yeah. Mostly about what you're going through. You know, on your weird days and the days you look like you're sick."

Dagon noticed all of that? He'd been watching me closer than I thought. "Did you tell him?"

"No," Zane assured me. "He's been worried about you, is all. So have we."

I took my beer and exited the kitchen, returned to pacing. "I've been fine."

"You've been worse, actually," Mack corrected. "I know you're not sleeping, and you're agitated all the time now."

"You would be too if you felt like you were having to swim through a pool of loud energies that were always shouting in your ears or emotions poking at you, making your skin crawl." I went to the windows and peered out over the commons below.

Since the day I was born, Mom said she knew I'd be different. Not in a "my kid's super special" way, but simply different. And damn if she wasn't right. Some of my earliest memories weren't of people's faces but of the glowing light around them or the way they made me feel. Our aunt said I was a sensitive, though she'd never had a chance to explain what that meant before she up and died in a car accident when I was eleven. Over the years, I realized I picked up on people's energy.

For a while, Mack thought I might be an empath, but it wasn't only a person's emotions I sensed. It was more like the essence of who they were as a person, down to their very core, would reach out and touch me whether I wanted to know about them or not.

Being around new people was the worst. I was accustomed to Zane and Mack. Most of the time, I could tune out their energies trying to talk to mine.

Then there were the other students. Thankfully, most of my classes were small. I picked my degree program in anthropology, with a focus on ancient religions as well as courses on metaphysics for two reasons. It was the program with the least amount of students, and I'd hoped somewhere along the way

I'd stumble across answers to what I was. Distance from people helped, but I'd found nothing aside from locking myself in a room kept the energies at bay. Or at least that used to work. Lately, there was no escape unless I was around Dagon.

The energy around him was unlike anything I'd experienced. It was like I stood beside a furnace that not only radiated heat but a fierce and unwavering will. At times, he gave off vibes of being a predator on the hunt. He didn't scare me. It was the opposite, actually. His energy seemed to cocoon me, shutting out everything else. He didn't even have to be close for me to feel the effects, just close enough.

The first day we met, his energy had sucked me in, right along with those hazel eyes of his. They were browner when he was agitated. That'd been most days these past few weeks. He had a sexy, roguish smile, but the stern look he'd adopted made it impossible not to notice the firm line to his jaw or the sharp cheekbones. The flannel shirts he wore all the time only added to his ruggedly handsome looks. His unruly black hair seemed to be an annoyance he'd come to live with, though he constantly ran his hands through it when he was frustrated.

"You think it's because of the murders?" Mack asked. "You being all wonky?"

I shrugged. It was a good guess, but it wasn't only the students' ramped-up anxiety over the recent deaths that made my life difficult. Zane might say Dagon was stressed because of his family, but I sensed there was far more going on in that head of his. Last night, he'd looked panicky even before he had his migraine attack. Afterward, he'd seemed ready to lose it. I shut my eyes, straining to recall every detail of what I'd witnessed. The claws, the horns, the way his hair lightened. His face had even shifted. The shimmering in his gaze had been beautiful and worrisome at the same time. And growling. There'd definitely been growling coming from him. His energy had turned into a maelstrom, swirling around us and crashing into me.

Then it ended as fast as it started.

I needed to talk to him. Too bad I sensed that was going to be nearly impossible now.

I finished my beer, told Mack and Zane I was heading out for the night, and went to the door a second time. Mack asked if I was sure I was alright. I waved off his concerns like I usually did, said I'd see them tomorrow, and headed out. The walk from their building to mine only took five minutes, but that was five minutes surrounded by unfamiliar energies that made me grit my teeth and walking as fast as I could without full-out sprinting to my door. Once inside my tiny studio apartment, I locked the door, kicked out of my sneakers, and waited for any semblance of peace to hit me.

While I waited for my heart to stop racing, I filled up the small watering can near my tiny kitchen area. The vining plants that lined the double window could use some water, as did all my little succulents covering several shelves around my bed. Each plant was supposed to promote calm and serenity.

It felt like a load of bullshit most days, but I was desperate for anything that would help me deal with what I went through daily. When I was younger, Mom had taken me to see a few different psychologists. None of them could give us any answers. There wasn't anything medically wrong with me. Over the years, I simply learned to tune out what I could and tolerate what I couldn't. I stopped being sociable and cut myself off from everyone as much as possible.

Mack might call me out for being a bookworm, but books didn't have emotions. They didn't have living energies. It wasn't the most extraordinary life, but at least I was keeping sane. I had my books and my plants. And my thoughts of Dagon.

A set of shimmering hazel eyes filled my mind,

followed by lips stretching into a grin right before they pressed to mine.

"Shit."

While daydreaming about Dagon, I'd overwatered one of my plants. I quickly wiped up the water flowing out of the pot. I didn't have Dagon. I wanted him, yeah, and after last night, I knew he wanted me, too. The question was, what kept holding him back?

"Gee, maybe it has to do with his having horns," I muttered to myself.

I spent the remainder of Friday night trying to get caught up on some essays and digging into a new paranormal paperback I'd picked up. When all that failed, I binge-watched one of my favorite ghost-hunting shows and eventually drifted to sleep.

THE SUN HIT my face way too early the following morning, and I groaned, yanking the blankets over my head. I'd hardly slept, my mind swarming with images of Dagon and his shifting face. He'd turned into a massive beast and swept me into his arms. I hadn't been afraid. Nothing made sense. Swiping my hands down my face, I rolled out of bed, freshened up in the bathroom, and was considering hiding inside all day until a knock sounded at the door.

Hoping somehow it was Dagon, I ran to open it and deflated at the sight of my friend Kayla.

"Wow, good morning to you too," she said with a laugh, holding out a paper cup of coffee from the campus café.

"Hey, sorry," I murmured, taking the coffee from her. "Forgot it was Saturday."

"You okay?"

Kayla stepped inside, carrying her dark blue yoga mat. Saturday mornings, we met up at my place to do a morning session, drink coffee, and relax. The energy around her was one of the reasons I'd introduced myself to her out of nowhere one day and asked if she'd ever want to hang out.

Her energy was so subtle, it was almost as good as being alone. I wasn't sure why, but I wasn't about to question it either. She was fun to hang out with and talk to. She wore brightly colored shirts all the time, along with flowing skirts, and I was certain she walked around barefoot when the weather was nice. Her dark blond hair was long and curly, hanging to her waist. I hardly ever saw her put it up unless we were doing yoga. She was so laid back, too. Mack had been ecstatic when I met her. She got me out of the library and my apartment more than he or Zane ever could.

One night, we'd been talking about our families. It was the only time I'd seen her sad. Her parents had been killed in an accident when she was little. The relatives who took her in had been good to her, but she didn't talk about them much. The last time I asked her about them at the beginning of the semester, she'd clammed up, saying there'd been some new family drama and hadn't wanted to bug me about it. I'd been worried about her, but she'd perked back up over the last couple of months.

"Yeah," I told Kayla, going to grab my purple yoga mat to lay next to hers on the floor. "Didn't sleep well. My back hurts this morning."

"We can do some deep stretching today. That might help."

Kayla taught weekly yoga classes for extra money and as part of her degree program. Our Saturdays also gave her a chance to try out new flows. I finished my coffee while she opened her notebook, talking to herself the entire time. She did that a lot.

"Right, here it is. You ready?"

I tossed the empty cup, stepped onto my mat, and we went through a thirty-minute long stretching session. As close as I'd become to Kayla, she had no idea about my sensitivity. She simply believed I suffered from a bad back. The yoga did help keep me in decent shape and relaxed my mind. As much as it could be relaxed.

At the end of the session, we sat on our mats, quietly meditating. My thoughts drifted until they were back on the reason I hadn't slept. Dagon. The grin he wore the night we met shifted into the severe frown he'd worn the last time I saw him. Horns appeared on his head, and when he opened his mouth, he had fangs, too. I jumped with a curse, shaking my head.

"Are you sure you're okay?" Eyes narrowed, Kayla studied me from her mat.

"Had weird dreams all night." It was about as close to the truth as I could get.

"Not surprised with all the crap going on around here." She hugged her knees to her chest, resting her chin on them. "Can't believe they found someone else dead. They're so close to campus. Scary to be out at night now."

"Guess so."

I probably should've been more afraid, what with people getting killed, but it was hard to be scared when everyone around was scared enough for all of us. I hadn't known the murder victims. It was tragic, but if I started letting my fear get to me, I'd never leave my apartment.

That, and knowing I had someone like Dagon watching over me from the shadows made me feel safer than I ever had before. The mystery of who he was had become an annoying itch. I needed to find a way to corner him and get some answers. Too bad I had to wait until tomorrow night before I could confront him.

It was going to be an exceptionally long day.

"What's with the look?"

I frowned. "What look?"

"That one right there. You seem awfully determined about something—and distracted." Kayla leaned over and nudged me. "Is it a guy? Please tell me it is. You could stand to go out on a date."

"Just thinking about Dagon."

Kayla scoffed, rising to her feet. "I don't know why you're still hung up on him."

Her harsh change in tone threw me off. "What do you mean? What's wrong with Dagon?"

"I just don't think he's the right guy for you." She rolled up her mat, her gaze fixed on the floor. "He flirts with you one time and then treats you like crap."

"He doesn't do that. He's polite, but distant. I think he's just worried about getting too close."

"That screams he's hiding something. It's been months. I think it's time you find some other guy to pine over. There's a whole college full of them. Take your pick. I could always set you up with someone. Could be a double date thing?"

The prospect of having to be around someone new wasn't appealing in the least bit. "I don't know. I'm not exactly down for a blind date."

"Then think of it as hanging out with new people. Casual drinks with friends."

I had no intention of giving up on Dagon, but Kayla was annoyingly persistent when she wanted to be. "Fine, but make sure the guy knows it's not a date. No pressure."

She squealed and hugged me. "I'll set it all up. We'll do Wilson's around eight on Monday?"

"Sounds like a plan."

"You'll like this guy, trust me. Much better than Dagon."

I bristled at her apparent dislike of Dagon, but she had her back turned and didn't notice. It didn't matter who she tried to set me up with. There was no getting over a guy who was turning out to have just as many weird secrets as I had.

4

DAGON

I parked my black Tahoe outside Jasmine and Arkon's farmhouse Saturday evening. The night before, I'd crashed at Calrod's place in Oak Hollow. He'd been out taking care of some handyman work around the town. Since moving here permanently, he took odd jobs here and there to seem legitimate. It was going to turn into a business soon enough if he kept it up. There hadn't been a chance to speak with him about the murders last night, and he'd been gone when I woke up this morning.

He'd left a note telling me to meet here tonight, and I could tell them all what was happening in Wellsville since they hadn't seen me since winter break. I'd texted him, hoping I could just talk to him and not get Arkon involved. All that did was make him worry more. If I didn't show tonight, they were coming to me even if I ran back to campus.

"Just remember," I told myself, climbing out of my vehicle, "you're only here to talk about the murders. Nothing else."

I let my glamour fall on my walk toward the front door. Arkon and Calrod's voices came from inside. I knocked, and the door flew open a second later.

"Was wondering if you were going to show." Arkon yanked me into a bear hug. I grunted, and he let me go, messing up the hair around my horns. "Where the hell have you been?"

"You know where." I endured another crushing hug from Calrod. "What's with you two? Not like I up and disappeared."

"It's been months," Arkon said, moving into the renovated living room.

More changes had been made to the house in my absence. The living room could now comfortably hold three full-sized demons in their natural state, as well as a handful of other people. The kitchen had also been redone, with the help of Calrod and Dylan, I assumed. The rear wall had been expanded, and a heavy-duty door was in place with three separate locks on it. All that appeared to be left to do were the two bedrooms and finishing the wrap-around front porch Arkon was determined to build so Jasmine could fully enjoy the view of the serene woods. He'd been going on about it for months. There was also the workshop he'd started out back, so she had more room to spread out her work for the antique store she ran. Just what she needed. More space to bring home more random shit. I'd heard Arkon complain more than once about how much stuff kept appearing at the house.

"You hardly call us anymore," Arkon scolded. "You're lucky we hadn't decided to drive out there and check on you."

"I'm fine. Just busy playing human."

Arkon and Calrod exchanged an aggravated look, crossed their arms, and stared at me. Their eyes glowed, and I cursed. This was exactly why I'd only wanted to drop in, talk to Calrod, then duck out. Lying to them through text or over the phone was easy. Doing it to their faces was nearly impossible. As long as I kept to the topic of the murders, I could get through tonight without spilling my guts about what had been going on since meeting Morgan.

"You want to spend all night grilling me, or can we discuss the six dead people in Wellsville?" I dug into my pocket for the amulet I found on the guy in the woods and tossed it onto the coffee table. "Starting to think they're being targeted for a particular reason."

Arkon picked up the necklace. "This had magic in it. Witches?"

"The last one was. I didn't get there in time to save him."

"Why would you have?" Calrod asked, then hung his head. "Shit. You've been seeing them."

I should've just told them all this over the damned phone. "I might've witnessed one of them about to die. Or all," I admitted when Calrod's eyes shimmered blue. "The last one was in a clearing next to a tree that was struck by lightning years ago. There was evidence of someone doing a ritual there. No idea if it's connected or not. The body had been ripped to pieces, just like the others."

"Rabid shifter?" Calrod suggested.

"I haven't picked up the trail of one. Whatever chased this guy down was massive. I heard it rushing toward him through the woods." I thought of the shadow-creature that attacked Morgan in my visions. My fangs lengthened, and I turned my back on my brothers, hiding my quickly growing claws, too. I'd witnessed the same two visions again this morning as if fate wanted to remind me why letting my guard down around her was a terrible idea.

"Dagon?"

"I'm fine," I uttered to Arkon.

"That growl says you're not," Calrod argued.

Shit, I *was* growling. I rolled my head on my neck, working to get myself under control. When I spun back around, I didn't have to read my brothers' thoughts to know what they were thinking. "Don't even start. I came here to talk about the murders, and that's all."

"You don't want to discuss why you've changed?"

"I haven't."

Arkon scoffed. "You're sure as hell not the same over-optimistic brother from a few months ago, and I doubt it all has to do with these murders. Even if these are witches, something else is bothering you. Don't need to be a psychic to know that." He leveled me with a scowl, daring me to challenge him. "What else is going on?"

"Nothing," I snarled, unable to stop myself from thinking of Morgan covered in blood. My claws and fangs were right back out again, and I curled my hands into tight fists. Putting a hole in the freshly painted blue walls would only serve to piss Jasmine off.

"Fuck, you are in trouble," Arkon muttered. When his lips curled in a grin then turned right back into a frown, I silently willed him to keep his revelation to himself. "You're acting exactly how I was when I first found Jasmine and realized she was in danger."

A flash of possessiveness followed by my fear of losing Morgan shot down my spine. I bared my fangs, not wanting Arkon or Calrod to know anything about her. She was mine and only mine. Arkon sighed in sympathy, and I reminded myself neither of my brothers was going to steal her from me.

"Who is she?" Calrod asked.

"Doesn't matter," I spat.

"Clearly it does if you're acting like this." Arkon's lips thinned, his eyes softening. "What kind of trouble is she in?"

I growled, unable to shake the images that had detonated in my mind. Morgan in danger. That shadow creature ready to devour her. Hearing her scream for me. Seeing her covered in blood. I smashed my hands to my face, yelling for it to stop.

"Don't tell me she's involved with the murders?" Calrod muttered. "Damn it, Dagon, why the hell didn't you call us sooner? Those started over a month ago."

"What's going on in here?" Jasmine's voice came from the hallway. My head shot up, catching her worried frown. "Dagon? Is it more bounty hunters?"

"No." Arkon took her hand and drew her into his arms. "And you don't need to worry about what it might be. You're supposed to be resting while you're sick."

"Sick?" I repeated. I'd talked to Arkon recently, hadn't I? Why didn't he say anything?

"Your brother's overreacting," Jasmine said.

"It's been over a week," Arkon argued. "You've had a fever off and on and you've been so tired. What do you expect me to do? Then that damned witch shows up and drags you into the bedroom to talk without me. I'm allowed to panic."

Cyrene was here, too? Shit. I hadn't been prepared to deal with the witch tonight, too, especially now that my secret was out.

"People get sick, you know," Jasmine said.

She did look like she was exhausted, but a smile tugged at her lips. Concern for her had me breaking my rule about reading the minds of my family members. She was brimming with excitement, and I gasped, clapping a hand over my mouth. Calrod and

Arkon eyed me funny, but I wasn't about to give away this news. My previous anger slipped away.

"It's a good thing you decided to build me a workshop. We're going to need it." Jasmine took one of Arkon's hands and pressed it to her stomach. "Surprise."

Arkon's face remained blank for a solid five seconds. Then his eyes widened, and he staggered back like he was about to fall over. "You're... I mean you're having," he fumbled over his words. "You're pregnant?"

"I'm pregnant," Jasmine whispered. "It's going to be a different kind of pregnancy since half-demon and all that. Explains the fever and feeling like shit and the tiredness, though I guess some of that's normal. Whatever. The point is I'm fine, and Cyrene promised she'll be here through all of it."

Arkon bundled her into his arms and kissed her. Even with my gift of visions, I hadn't seen this one coming. Jasmine laughed, and Arkon picked her up, spinning her around. I never thought I'd see him happy again. Now he had the love of his life at his side, he had a home, and soon he'd have a family. A baby. They were having a baby together.

It was like someone dumped a bucket of ice water over my head. I never should've come here tonight. The last thing Arkon and Jasmine needed in their lives now was more trouble. If I told them anymore, I'd be bringing untold horrors right to their doorstep. It wasn't only the murderer running loose that had my stomach twisting in knots. The shadow-creature after Morgan could be an entirely different monster. One sent by Prince Carridan. There was always a chance he'd found out we were alive. Until I knew what was after Morgan, I needed to stay as far away from Oak Hollow as possible.

"Congratulations," I told Arkon and Jasmine. "I'm happy for you both, really, but I should go."

"You just got here." Jasmine came toward me.

I immediately moved back. "It's better if I stay away. I can handle this on my own."

"It's true then," Cyrene called, joining us in the living room. "You three all carry the same notion that you have to do everything on your own. And here, I'd hoped the youngest of you would be smarter than that."

Gritting my teeth, I shifted my gaze to the witch with long, violet hair. "Cyrene."

"Dagon. It's been far too long, wouldn't you say?" She stepped into the living room, and her flowing skirt made up of various pieces of jaggedly cut fabric dragged on the ground behind her. The matching blue top she had was made of the same material, making her look as if she stepped out of a painting from some fantasy world.

"It's good to see you, but I shouldn't be here."

"Is it because of the murders or because of what you've been seeing?" she asked.

I froze with my hand on the front door. "Don't," I warned, sensing my anger creeping in again.

"What's she talking about?" Calrod stomped toward me, forcibly removing my hand from the door. "What have you been hiding from us?"

"I can't," I shouted, tearing myself out of his grasp. "Not now."

"I know what you're doing. Don't you dare use me as a reason to stop telling your brothers shit," Jasmine said, pointing her finger at me. "We're family. Whatever's going on, you need to tell us so we can help you and you can stop falling apart."

"I'm not falling apart."

Jasmine barked a laugh. "Yeah, sure you're not. That's why you look like shit. And sound awful and look ready to tear something apart with your bare hands."

"I think he found his mate," Arkon told her, and she beamed at me.

"She's not my mate," I snarled. "She can't be, so just let it go. I never should've come here."

"You've seen her die," Cyrene said, and it was like someone stabbed me in the heart then twisted the blade. "More than once, too. You've seen her covered in blood, calling out for you."

"Stop," I whispered, the ache in my chest spreading.

"You've seen the monster come from the shadows to take her away."

"I said stop." I bellowed, charging across the living room, my claws and fangs bursting free of my control.

Grabbing Cyrene's shoulder, I slammed her into the wall and raised my hand, ready to make her shut up. Her eyes glowed violet in warning, and her skin tingled with magic which was waiting to attack. There was no fear, however. None.

"I've seen it, too."

"What? What did you say?" I lowered my hand but didn't release her.

"You're not the only one cursed with the gift of visions. Come, I think it's far past time we sit down for a little chat. And if you even try to leave, I'll bring you right back," she threatened. "There's something dark at work in the town of Wellsville. You're going to help me stop it, so is Morgan."

"No, she can't have anything to do with this mess," I whispered. "I won't lose her to that monster. It's safer if she stays away."

"Is that truly what you believe? You're more of a fool than Arkon."

I considered arguing, but she was already marching to the kitchen. Calrod gave me a helpful shove in that direction, and I traipsed after her. Arkon and Jasmine hung back in the living room, talking quietly with their heads together. He kissed her forehead, wrapping her in his arms, both of them grinning. He ran his hands lightly up and down her arms, and she buried her face against his chest, squeezing him tightly.

I willed a vision to come, anything to tell me I wasn't about to screw up what my brother had finally found.

But there was no helpful message, no vision, only a growing sense of dread that I was about to drag all of us into a fight that wasn't going to end in our favor.

THE ONLY SOUND in the kitchen was the ticking of an antique wall clock in the shape of a satyr. I'd heard the story about why Jasmine thought it was hysterical and a great reminder of how Arkon came back into her life. Calrod's chair scooted across the tile floor, and his hand connected with the back of my head. I growled, only to have Arkon do the exact same thing.

"You're a dumbass," Arkon muttered with his hit. "Why didn't you tell us when this shit started?"

I rubbed the back of my head, glowering at him. "Maybe because you were still off trying to get yourself killed, and Calrod was spending all his time making sure you didn't die."

"That's no excuse," Arkon snapped. "I would've come to help you if you'd asked me to."

"Look," I said, pushing back from the round kitchen table to pace around the room, "I didn't tell you guys because I thought I could handle it on my own. I didn't expect to keep seeing the same visions of her over and over until they'd begun to drive me crazy. Or start to change into something worse." I paused by the sink, staring out the window over it.

Jasmine's garden was freshly turned over with a few plants coming in. A fierce longing to have a place to call home hit me hard. All these years, I'd told myself I didn't need a single place to live, a way to put down roots. Now, all of that changed. I shut my eyes, and there was Morgan's smiling face waiting for me. She was what I wanted to see every day, to hold in my arms. To kiss. I opened my eyes, staring at my shimmering-eyed reflection in the window.

"I just don't understand why I'm seeing these visions of her and the murders. If this killer is targeting witches, it has nothing to do with her. It can't have anything to do with her," I said, spinning around.

Cyrene tapped her sparkling blue nails on the table, her face unreadable.

"She's not a witch," I said. "She's different, but I'd know if she were a witch."

"Are you sure?" Cyrene asked. "Witches come in many different forms. The way it sounds, Morgan Nelson could very well have magic in her veins." She rose abruptly, grinning. "I'd like to meet her."

"What? No," I snapped with a guttural growl. "She's not getting anywhere near our world."

"Bit late for that," Cyrene said with a gentle laugh. "You want her, don't you? Those feelings aren't simply going to go away. Ask your brother."

"She's not wrong. You can't keep fighting your

instincts." Arkon reached for Jasmine's hand, pulling her into his arms. "Trust me."

"It's not the same," I whispered. "You didn't see her getting killed in a vision stuck on repeat."

Arkon's hand drifted to the spot just below Jasmine's sternum, and I wanted to bite back the words I'd said. "You're right. But I did watch her die. I almost lost her. It still terrifies me some nights that some other asshole is going to show up to steal her from me. And now with the baby," he let out a heavy breath, and Jasmine gently patted his cheek. He kissed her hand, hugging her close. "You wanted us to find a way to live, find happiness and love, remember? It's time you do the same for yourself."

This was not the same demon I'd known since we were exiled from the Underworld. Jasmine had done so much for Arkon, more than she'd probably ever realize.

"Fear is a part of living," Cyrene said. "It's a part of loving."

"Love?" I sputtered. "I never said anything about love."

"No? Then what do you call being a silent protector all this time?" Cyrene said with a smile. "That's love, whether you want to accept it or not. Now," she clapped her hands, sending blue and violet sparks shooting into the air, "I expect to meet this Morgan in the next couple of weeks. I can help her understand what she is, ease some of her discomfort she seems to be in all the time. And as far as this murderer going around killing witches, you are to alert me the next time you have a vision, understand?" She handed me a card she pulled out of thin air with a number on it. "Do not try to track them down alone."

"And the monster in my vision?" I shoved the card in my pocket. "The beast that kills Morgan?"

She hesitated, then said, "They could very well be one and the same. You keep an eye on her. Protect her as you've been doing, and I promise you, we'll find a way to keep her alive. Both of you." She stepped back, observing my brothers, me, and Jasmine. "Destiny is far from being finished with you lot." With one final bow of her head, she twisted her hand in the air. A leaf-filled gust of wind erupted in the kitchen. It swarmed around her, and then she was gone.

"Be nice if she'd take the leaves with her," Arkon muttered.

"Could be worse," Jasmine said with a grin. "Could be demon guts all over the walls again."

"You're insane. You know that?" Arkon kissed

her, cutting off her protests. "And you," he added, turning to me, "you're staying here tonight, so we can talk more about this Morgan of yours."

"Yeah, Cyrene's not the only one who wants to meet her." Jasmine started to make a pot of coffee.

I gave in, slouching in a chair at the table.

She measured the grounds. "Don't look so glum. We're not that terrible to be around."

Calrod muttered a few choice words about Arkon being the worst of us all. They bantered with Jasmine chiming in now and then. The doom and gloom that had gripped me since that first vision of Morgan shattered bit by bit until it was washed away by a surge of relief at someone knowing the truth. Calrod clapped me on the shoulder, and Arkon ruffled my hair until I was shoving his hand away and laughing. Jasmine came to me, too, giving me a squeeze.

"We need happy Dagon back. After all, you're about to be an uncle."

Arkon froze, his eyes widening. Then they softened, and he turned away, swiping at his face. They might have agreed to help me save Morgan and stop the murderous rampage in Wellsville, but once we figured out who was behind it, I'd be going after them on my own. Arkon had far too much to lose now.

Jasmine brought the coffee over and Calrod put in an order for pizza.

I settled in at the kitchen table and started to tell them about the woman I couldn't stop thinking about.

5

MORGAN

I knocked on Zane's door, calling his name. All his text said was I needed to get over there. Mack's had, too. Neither had replied when I asked what was going on. They didn't answer my calls either.

"Seriously, guys, if this is some prank, I'm going to kick both your asses," I yelled through the door. "Not in the mood for this shit tonight. I already had a horrible day, so if you don't get out here in the next three seconds—"

The door opened, but it wasn't Mack or Zane on the other side. A rush of heat followed immediately by the sensation that I was cut off from the rest of the world struck me. My shoulders slumped in relief from the energy swirling around my body.

"Dagon," I breathed.

"I'd really like you not to kick my ass."

Dagon's eyes shimmered with amusement, though there was no smile on his face. The black flannel shirt he wore was undone, revealing a white t-shirt underneath. The sleeves were rolled up, high-lighting his toned forearms and showing the tattoos of words in a language I didn't recognize. They started at his wrists and circled up his arms, disap-pearing beneath the sleeves. He wore those damned snug jeans, and he was barefoot. I licked my lips, unable to stop my gaze from slipping to his mouth. My dreams last night had featured Dagon and me, and we weren't exactly talking.

"Morgan?"

"Uh, sorry, I just—" I shook my head, clearing my throat. "Is Zane here? Or Mack?"

"Haven't seen them since I've been back."

I was going to strangle those two the next time I saw them. "Well, didn't mean to interrupt your evening. I'll see you around or something." So much for making him talk to me. Nerves got the better of me, and I turned to go, hating to leave the comforting energy of Dagon.

"Morgan," he said, stopping me in my tracks. "Wait, I want to apologize for the other night."

The other night.

I spun around, jumping when I saw Dagon's face shift and horns appear atop his head. A door slammed down the hall, and I gritted my teeth at the influx of energies that crowded the hallway from the group of students headed our way. They closed in around me, bringing with them a tidal wave of emotions I had no hope of shutting out. A warm hand took hold of mine and tugged me forward. Another door closed, and that same hand slid up my arm to hold my shoulder.

"Are you alright? Morgan?"

The chaotic energy from the hall slipped away and was replaced by a cocoon of warmth that was all Dagon. The same fierce will was there, but with it was another emotion I hadn't expected. Desire so powerful and complete stole the last bit of air from my lungs. I forgot to breathe. My head spun, and two arms caught me up at the same time my knees gave out.

"Easy," Dagon whispered, holding me to him.

"You," I murmured, shaking my head and failing to get the rest of the words out. My eyes fluttered open to stare right into those shining hazel depths that filled my dreams. "Different."

Dagon's eyes crinkled. "What's different?"

"You," I repeated. "Why do you feel like this?"

"I don't understand what you mean."

I shoved out of his arms, trying to get a grip. My palms were sweaty, and my heart raced. Dagon closed the door to the apartment, keeping a wary eye on me the whole time. For nine months, I'd grown accustomed to sensing Dagon's specific energy, the calming balm it was to the craziness around me. There'd been the strength and an unbreakable will, the sensation of being near a watchful predator. Now, though, that had all changed. His energy sought me out intentionally, reaching around me with invisible bonds of attraction, undeniable want, and was that fear? Never in all the time I'd known him had I caught even a hint of these emotions. Where the hell had they come from? Had he been holding them back from me all this time?

The desire was like a caress down my spine, and I rolled my head on my shoulders, not wanting it to stop. An answering wave of yearning rose in me. It built until I had no choice but to imagine it breaking free.

Dagon grunted, clutching his hand to his chest. He sucked in a sharp breath, then another, his eyes seeming to glow.

This was crazy. No one could feel like this, could

they? And what was I even doing? I'd never been able to release energy like that before, but from the way he reacted, that was precisely what I'd just done. I took a tentative step toward Dagon, and he did the same. A tingling started at my temples, followed by another torrent of passion that I couldn't honestly discern if it was from him or me. My body was on fire. I had to get closer to him. The tiny space left between us disappeared, and impulsively, I reached for his hand.

An electric shock shot up my arm at the contact. I waited for Dagon to take his hand back, but it remained in mine. The apartment became much smaller, and the heat that followed him pressed in around me like I was bundled up in bed. I sank into the sensation. My eyes closed, and my fingers wandered, trailing over Dagon's palm, then his wrist, and back down to his knuckles. I told myself to stop being weird but being this close to him muddled my rational thinking process. The same rumbling growl I'd thought I heard the other night sounded, and my eyes flew open. The green flecks in his irises burned brighter than should've been possible. He guided me backward, moving until the edge of the kitchen counter bumped into me. His hands slipped up my arms to my elbows, holding me between the countertop and his body shimmering with the same energy as his eyes.

His gaze wandered over my face then lower to my rapidly rising and falling chest. The V-neck dark purple t-shirt I wore wasn't anything special, nor were the boyfriend-cut jeans I had on, but his lips curled into a smile all the same. The glistening in his eyes brightened, and his face seemed to shift beneath the kitchen lights. A white scar appeared on the right side of his jaw. The firm curve to his cheeks shifting had to be the shadows playing tricks on my mind. His lips, god, his lips were full, enhancing his already handsome features. I pinched my tongue between my teeth, wanting nothing more than to kiss him and see how warm those lips would be.

The next second, Dagon's hand buried itself in my hair, the other snagged my hip, and he slanted his mouth over mine. He was far warmer than I expected. I sighed, pressing my lips firmly to his. When I parted my lips, he groaned, and his tongue slipped inside, deepening the kiss. The temperature rose impossibly more until I expected to be on fire. His hand at my hip held me in place, but I wanted more. I shifted my body closer, eager to see where this would go.

As fast as the kiss started, he drew back, his brow

wrinkled and his lips red. "Sorry. That was too much. Was it too much? I feel like it was."

I shrugged, unsure myself of what we were both experiencing right then. "Maybe?"

"Right, yeah." He started to step away, but I dragged him right back into my embrace.

His hand squeezed my hip, then slid around to cup my ass. I snagged hold of his flannel shirt, dragging him as close as he could get. Kissing Dagon was like giving in to a craving I hadn't even known existed within me.

I sucked on his tongue. His hand moved down my body, outlining my curves. A shiver of sheer pleasure shot down my back. He did it again, both hands feeling me up from my back, around my ribcage, then to my ass. My thighs clenched together, imagining giving in to several of the fantasies that had been rambling around in my mind since meeting Dagon.

His arousal pressed into my stomach through his jeans. I reached down, pressing my hand to the bulge, the heat in my lower belly intensifying at how hard and ready he was for me. He cursed against my mouth, his hips bucking gently. His hand just reached up to my breast, heavy with desire, when he broke the kiss a second time and backed much further away. He swiped a hand down his face, fighting to catch his breath.

I pressed my fingers to my tingling lips them while the rest of my body leaned forward as if pulled to Dagon. He cleared his throat, rubbing the back of his neck. "I—uh, I don't know what got into me," he whispered, his voice husky.

"Same," I replied quietly.

What was going on with me tonight? I hadn't intended to see Dagon until tomorrow, if that, and here I was making out with him in his kitchen.

"You're different," I said, telling myself that this time, I'd get further than those two words.

"I'm still not sure what you mean."

"I think you do. Why did you just kiss me like that?"

"I could ask you the same thing."

"Dagon," I said, and he blew out a breath, running his hands madly through his hair. "Can you just talk to me? Give me some answers for once? I think you owe me that much."

His face fell into a severe frown I hated seeing on him. Then it gave way to an apologetic smile. "I know I've been distant since we've met, and I'm sorry for that. I was stupid and afraid, and I didn't want to let myself get close to you because I knew this would happen," he rambled, waving his hand between us.

My lips still feeling the heat from his made it hard to focus. The fervent pulsing of emotions wasn't helping either. "This whole time, you've wanted to be with me?" I managed to ask.

"Yeah," he said with a nervous laugh. "I thought it'd be better for you if I stayed away."

"Why do you make it sound like you're some horrible person?"

His eyes had yet to break their hold on mine. They darkened, and his face seemed to blur again, but only for a second. I shook my head, trying to clear the haze, and Dagon was back to normal. "There's a lot about my family and me I can't tell you yet. Not that I don't trust you, it's just difficult to explain. The last thing I want is to drag you into it. You have enough to deal with."

How did he know what I had to go through every day? Zane said he hadn't told Dagon anything about my being sensitive.

"I notice things," he explained quietly as if reading my mind. "You have a lot of bad days. The hiding in your room. Not socializing. The discomfort when you're around a lot of people."

"Unless they're you," I said, then clapped a hand over my mouth.

His lips twitched. "Me?"

There was no point in trying to hide it now, I supposed, not that I was in any mood to even attempt to describe what I went through daily. "You're different from everyone else. I don't know why, but you are. That's not the only reason I like you, by the way," I added in a rush, and he chuckled.

"Glad to hear it." His smile widened, lighting up his eyes and crinkling the skin around them in the most adorable way. I hadn't seen him grin like that since the first night we met.

"Do I amuse you?" I asked.

"More than that," he said, striding back to me one agonizingly gradual step at a time. "You, Morgan Nelson, fascinate the hell out of me. You always have."

"Is that so?" The words came out breathy, and I nibbled on my bottom lip, craving him all over again. There was no time to question what was going on with me, and I didn't care to. I snagged him by his shirt and yanked him to me.

Our bodies collided in a raging storm that had no end in sight. I'd never wanted to possess someone so entirely or have the same done to me in turn.

Whatever concerns I had about being with Dagon vanished, leaving me open and simply knowing I had to have him touching me. Holding me. He growled quietly, kissing down my neck to my collar bone. I ran my hands through his hair, lightly massaging his scalp. My hands neared his forehead, and his arm tightened around me. He devoured my mouth, his tongue driving me crazy. His hand moved exactly how I wanted it to, cupping my breast and massaging it. When his thumb caressed my hardened nipple through my shirt, I shivered, forgetting I'd spent the last nine months worried I'd read the signs all wrong.

My hips reacted to the flood of emotions curling around me, pressing into him. His swollen shaft was right there to greet me. His hands fell to my hips, and he ground against me. My toes curled in my shoes, and I wound my arms around his neck, deepening the kiss impossibly more. Clothes. Why were we still wearing clothes?

His lips slowed their fervent kisses, and he rested his forehead to mine. "We should, uh, we should slow down," he said in between gasps for air. "No need to rush this."

"You sure about that? You're not going to change your mind on me tomorrow?"

He bucked his hips gently into me, and I dragged my nails down his chest, fisting my hands in the flannel. "Not even close. I want to date you, amongst other things. I was a scared fool all these months."

"And now?"

"Still scared, but I can't stay away from you, not any longer." He cupped my face and barely let his lips touch mine. "What are you doing tomorrow night?"

"Tomorrow? What's tomorrow? Damn, what's today?" We laughed, and he kissed me again.

"Tomorrow is Monday."

I started to say I was free, then sighed. "I have something going on tomorrow night with a friend. I could cancel." Kayla would give me never-ending shit for it if I did, but if I got to see Dagon, it was worth it.

"No, I don't want to take over your life."

"If you're sure," I said slowly, and he nodded. "I'm free the rest of the week. Just tell me when."

"Trust me, I will." He gently lifted my chin, studying me with one narrowed eye. "You still having a rough day?"

"No, I think I'll be okay." I longed to stay, but the urge to tackle him to the closest soft surface clouded my mind again. He breathed in and out heavily through his nose, our emotions a tangled mess. I needed to take a breather, give myself time to think. Give us both time to clear our heads and figure out what we were doing. "I'm going to head back to my place."

"Want me to walk you?" He glanced toward the windows, but it was still light out.

"I'll be okay."

"Text me when you get inside."

"Such a worrywart," I teased, and he scowled. "I will, promise."

He released me, and I walked to the door on unsteady feet, only this time, it wasn't from my back aching so bad I wanted to cry. That was how it'd been before I'd come over here, and Dagon had opened the door. Someone had leaked details about how the latest murder victim was found. Fear and panic were rampant. I'd spent all day struggling to stop the emotions and negative energies from driving me crazy.

It took everything I had not to find a reason to stay with Dagon. I smiled at him one last time, then exited the apartment. On the walk back to mine, I waited for Dagon's energy to slip away and leave me. It lingered, bolstering my strength and blocking out the noisiness I'd grown accustomed to dealing with when strolling across campus. I wasn't able to stop smiling or feeling his hands. Even his woodsy scent of mint and pine stayed with me all the way to my apartment.

I unlocked the door, stepped inside, and texted Dagon. He said he'd see me tomorrow in class and to have a good night. I sent another message to Mack and Zane, informing them I hated them as much as I loved them for setting me up. They bombarded me with questions, but I ignored them. They'd just have to wait to get answers. Tossing my cell on my bed, I kicked out of my shoes and sighed.

"So you made out with him," I muttered. "And it was hot and sexy, and you want to do it all over again. It has been a while. A long, long while."

Shit, when was the last time I'd made out with a guy? Over a year? No, it was further back than that. No wonder I was all over him. That's all these crazy urges that were shooting through my mind. I was just a horny twenty-five-year-old. I thought it, but I knew being around Dagon was awakening more than random passion. This was more intense. Stronger.

And a hell of a lot riskier for both of us. His worries about dragging me into his troubles remained a quiet, nagging voice in the back of my mind. One day soon, I sensed Dagon and I were going to have a not-so-pleasant conversation about who he was. Hell, who we both were.

I changed into the oversized blue t-shirt I used as a nightgown, flipped out the lights, and fell into bed. Most nights, it took forever to relax and fall asleep, thanks to the residual energies clinging to me from my day. Then there were the energies pressing in from everyone else in the building.

Tonight, though, all I felt was the enduring essence of Dagon. The ghost of his touch drifted over my body. The way he'd held me, kissed me, it was like he knew exactly how my body wanted to be touched. I bit my lip, sinking into the warmth he'd left behind. Sleep crept in, and I grinned, my imagination taking off with me and wondering what the next few days would bring.

WHY DIDN'T I just tell Kayla I didn't want to go out tonight? I'd been at Wilson's bar, the local hangout for college students, since eight. The two guys she brought with her were friends from one of her classes. I hated to admit I didn't recall their names and hadn't exactly been making much of an attempt to socialize.

Kayla and the one with short dark hair were currently flirting it up at our high-top table. The one she silently claimed as her date for the night had bright eyes and a smile that was beyond charming. They were getting along great. The other guy, shit, what was his name? Kevin? That sounded right. We'd been keeping up a polite conversation most of the night while we sipped on our beers.

The bar wasn't crowded, but the number of people here was more than enough to leave me gritting my teeth. I peeled the beer label free and proceeded to tear it up.

Kayla and her date got up, laughing hysterically, and started a game of darts.

"So," Kevin said, "going to guess this wasn't your idea."

I cringed. "I'm sorry. Kayla's about my only girlfriend, and she seemed really excited about tonight."

"It's okay," he assured me. "Alex is the same. I came for moral support."

I lifted my beer in a toast, and he clinked his against mine. "Cheers to being a moral support system for our friends while they navigate the harrowing experience that is dating in your twenties."

"Think that's the longest toast I've ever toasted to." Kevin laughed with me, and we drank our beers until they were empty. "Another round?"

"Yeah, that'd be nice."

Kevin grinned and went to fetch two more beers from the bar. I let out a quick sigh of relief. This evening might not be so horrible as I thought. Kevin was a nice enough guy, but I hadn't been able to stop thinking about Dagon since I woke up this morning. I might've told him I had plans tonight, but it was only a little after nine. Maybe when I could finally leave without aggravating Kayla, I'd text Dagon and see if he was still awake. Going to his place would mean bumping into Zane. Possibly my brother, too. I really didn't want to wait until tomorrow to see him again, though. It'd been hard enough to make it through our class today. He'd changed his seat to the one right beside me.

I spent the entire two hours thinking about kissing him.

A few more people entered the bar, and I shifted in my seat at the pressure building around me.

"You okay?" Kevin asked, returning with two more beers.

"Yeah, just thinking about classes."

The doors opened, and even more students came in. This time the energy surge left a bitter taste in my mouth. My back ached like it usually did on the days I was surrounded by a lot of negative emotions. With the murders taking place in Wellsville, that was almost every class now.

But what I sensed now wasn't fear. This was something else. Something worse.

"Morgan?"

I turned to Kevin, confused about why he looked so worried. I blinked, realizing I was on my feet and had already taken a few steps toward the doors to leave. "Uh, sorry. I have to use the bathroom. I'll be right back."

I spun around and weaved through the bar to the short hall leading to the bathrooms. My arm brushed someone else's on the way, and I gasped at the stabbing anxiety in my stomach. The guy shot me a smile that was more of a sneer. I picked up the pace and ducked into the single bathroom, locking the door behind me.

"Get a grip," I whispered to my reflection, then splashed cold water on my face.

I'd been around Dagon today, but not enough for his energy to linger as it had last night. I shut my eyes, straining to find a hint of it anywhere near or on me. Holding my breath and scrunching my eyes shut did nothing but leave me light-headed and curling my hands tighter around the porcelain sink. Nothing. Not even a blip of Dagon was on me.

I never should've agreed to come out tonight.

Kayla would have to forgive me later. If I stayed here much longer, it'd be impossible to plaster a fake smile on my face. I wasn't in the mood to deal with a massive backache all night, either. Another rush of energy left my head spinning, and I nearly lost the beer I'd drunk. Once I was sure I wasn't going to vomit all over Kevin, I straightened and thought of an excuse to give to Kayla. My stomach churned, and I decided explanations were best left for tomorrow.

I had to get out of here. Whoever was in this bar tonight was trouble, and trouble wasn't what I needed to deal with right now.

"What's got you in a tizzy?"

I frowned at Zane from across the living room. "Huh?"

"You keep stomping around the apartment, brooding," he pointed out from his spot on the couch. "And muttering under your breath."

"Sorry. Just uh, didn't sleep well," I admitted, rubbing my eyes.

After Morgan left last night, I hadn't been able to fall asleep. The desire to go after her and have her back in my arms had been overwhelming. I'd let down my walls alright, but I'd never expected to be swept away in the storm that was Morgan, not that passionately.

Not that completely.

There'd been nothing that mattered more than touching her in those few moments. Seeing her today had been a sweet torture I wasn't sure I'd be able to endure tomorrow. Arkon had warned me it'd be impossible to ignore my feelings for long. I supposed suppressing them all these months meant they were coming across far more potent than I intended. The way Morgan reacted to a simple touch, to merely being in the same room with me, had left me breathless.

When I'd finally passed out last night, all I'd dreamt about was her with me beneath the sheets while she moaned and whispered my name. This morning, I'd still felt her mouth against me, like she was right there in bed beside me. I cursed, taking another lap around the apartment. I'd let myself slip into her thoughts during our kissing last night. I'd tumbled down so fast into a burning fire of desire that only fueled mine even more.

"Did something happen yesterday?" Zane asked.

I stopped short, not about to tell him how I'd made out with Morgan and probably would've gone further if the rational side of my mind hadn't kicked in. I longed to do so much more with her. So much more. It'd been nearly impossible to not only stay out of her thoughts during our class but to stop myself from leading her into the nearest empty classroom to play out what we both had in mind last night.

"No," I grated out, and Zane laughed. "What?"

"You're saying nothing happened at all? You sure?"

"Why are you so interested?"

He stood up, slinging his backpack onto his shoulder. "Just saying if anything had happened between you and a certain someone, you could say thank you."

"Why do you want to set us up so badly?"

He shrugged, making his way to the door. "What can I say? I like being cupid."

"Zane, seriously.'

"What? You like her, man. You've liked her since day one. I don't know what's been stopping you unless you're that worried about the whole mind-reading thing. I can tell you right now, Morgan won't care. She's crazy about you, too. Mack and I just thought we'd give you both a little nudge."

"Hey," I said, and he paused in the doorway, "thanks."

He winked. "Anytime."

"Where you off to?"

"Study group. I'll probably be out late or might

not come back at all." His cheeks reddened, and it was my turn to wink.

"Let me guess, Anthony's in this group."

"He might be."

"Maybe take your own advice then," I threw at him, and he laughed.

"Maybe I will." He waved, and the front door closed with a solid thud behind him.

I pulled my cell from my pocket but shoved it right back. I wasn't sure what Morgan was up to tonight, and sending her a bunch of texts would be obnoxious. It was after nine anyway. For all I knew, she could be back in her apartment and tucked in for the night. Picturing her lying in bed set off an avalanche of fantasies I had no hope of stopping.

What did she sleep in? I grinned, doubting she was much for fancy pajamas. What if she slept naked with nothing but a sheet draped over her bare skin? My hands curled, and I growled, glad Zane had gone out for the night. My jeans became uncomfortable, and I figured I might as well put on comfier clothes and crash for the night.

A searing pain shot across my forehead, nearly sending me to my knees. I pressed the heels of my palms to my eyes while images assaulted my mind. Morgan's face appeared; music played in the background. She stood down the sidewalk, just down from Wilson's bar. There were a couple of guys standing to her right. One of them grabbed her arm, and she raised her hand to hit him. He sneered and tried to drag her down the sidewalk. The vision cut off before I got the chance to see anything else. Using the wall, I clawed my way upright and sprinted for the door.

Wilson's was a couple of blocks away from campus. My visions never gave me a time frame. For all I knew, Morgan was already dealing with those two assholes. I growled, seeing one of them lay a hand on her all over again. The students I'd been walking beside jumped and stepped off the sidewalk to get away from me. My glamour was barely holding, but I wasn't about to stop to reinforce the spell.

Morgan. I had to get to Morgan.

The sign for Wilson's Bar lit up the front walk and the door beneath it. Morgan was nowhere in sight, and neither were the two guys. I flashed my ID to the bouncer at the door and ducked inside. I hoped she hadn't left yet, but there was no sign of her in the bar. Cursing harsh enough to draw more attention, I stomped right back outside and stalked down the sidewalk. Shutting my eyes, I let my mind seek out those around me. When I landed inside a stream of panic followed immediately by anger, I took off in that direction. Morgan. She wasn't going to run. She was going to try to beat up the assholes herself.

"I said get off, jackass!"

I followed Morgan's scream from around the side of the bar and lost all thought of keeping my true identity a secret. I snarled, barreling into the two guys crowding Morgan against the wall. They skidded down the asphalt, slamming into each other on their way down. Too caught up with protecting Morgan, I didn't stop myself from peering into their minds. What they wanted to do to her had my anger spiking impossibly more. I planted myself in front of Morgan, the glamour slipping. My claws extended, and I bared my fangs, snarling at the two guys after they made it back to their feet.

"What the fuck, man?" the taller one shouted, then gulped. His eyes bulged, and he shoved his friend in front of him. "What are you?"

I opened my mouth, but all that came out was a throaty growl. I snapped my jaws, swiping at them. They fell back, scrambling to not be the one in front. The muscles in my neck and arms bulged, and I stood at my full height.

"Mine," I snapped. "Touch her again, and I'll rip your fucking heads off."

The guy in front with the large nose shook. I took a step closer, growling, and he yelped. The front of his pants grew wet, and he yelled, turning and taking off around the building. The one who'd grabbed Morgan was right behind him. I considered chasing them and really giving them a fright, but a hand snagged my arm. I whirled around with a growl, but it was only Morgan. Her eyes skimmed over my face, then higher. I willed the glamour back into place, but it didn't stick. I turned away, not wanting Morgan to see me like this, but she didn't let go of my arm. Her hand slipped into mine, and she squeezed it.

"Hey, I'm okay," she said, shifting so she could look into my eyes. "I'm alright."

The anxiety of not reaching her in time dissipated slightly, but not enough to gain control of my burning anger. I was entranced and confused at how she wasn't losing her mind with fright at what I was. My eyes danced over her makeup-less face, searching for a hint of unease. There was none. Her hair was a bit messy, a few strands hanging around her face. The chunky bracelets at her wrist today were onyx and lapis lazuli, matching her dark blue t-shirt. Her right ear was adorned with her usual neon dinosaur studs. Gods, she was beautiful in her fierce-ness. If I didn't know any better, I'd say I was looking at a demon myself.

"Dagon, I'm okay," Morgan repeated, her hands sliding up my tensed arms to my shoulders.

I breathed out heavily through my nose. She had no idea what those bastards had wanted to do to her. No idea at all. But I did. I could see it plain as day.

"Dagon," Morgan said sternly, and my eyes flicked to her.

She didn't look afraid. How was she not? Not even her thoughts were consumed with worry for herself. That was reserved for me. I shook my head, attempting to work the glamour spell again, but it wouldn't come.

"Can't hide it," I whispered.

She glanced at my horns again. "We need to get you inside." She had her oversized tote bag with her and pulled out a fleece jacket with a hood. "Might look stupid but put this on over your head at least. No one should notice anything else."

I did as she said, too numb by her reaction to my appearance to do much else. That, and I was still contemplating chasing after those two pieces of shit to teach them a more thorough lesson. Once the hood was in place, Morgan gave me a quick once over, nodded, and tugged me along behind her. We walked quickly, not saying a word the entire walk back to the apartment buildings on campus. We darted up the steps to the third floor, where her place was. She unlocked the door and shoved me inside ahead of her. The lights flipped on, and she tossed her tote bag to the floor by the door.

I removed the fleece jacket, laying it over the back of the loveseat. She came toward me, and I moved away, holding up a hand bearing black claws. They'd shrunk a bit, but I couldn't get them to retract all the way. "Stay there."

"You won't hurt me."

A quiet growl rumbled through my chest. "How are you not losing it right now?"

"I might've seen you like this already," she replied.

"What? When?"

"The other night, before you had a migraine attack. Your horns sort of shimmered into view, and your face changed." She planted her hands on her hips, tilting her head. "So, this is the real Dagon. What are you?"

All I could do for a solid ten seconds was stare at her. When reality kicked in that I wasn't hiding my true face from her any longer, and she wasn't running for the door screaming, I grunted. "Demon. Why didn't you run?"

"Why would I do that?"

I waved a hand over myself. "Why do you think?"

She shrugged, picking at her nails and studying the floor while she shifted on her feet. "I told you, you won't hurt me."

"You can't know that."

"With you I can," she argued. Her eyes skipped to mine, and I chanced a glance inside her mind. There was curiosity and way too many questions for me to even contemplate starting to answer tonight. She was shaken up by those guys grabbing her, but that was it. "Demon. Demons are real?"

"Obviously," I said, and she laughed.

"Right, yeah. Sorry, that was a stupid question."

"Don't be sorry," I snapped, trying and failing once again to get my glamour back in place. "Those assholes should be sorry." My lip twitched, and I stalked around her apartment. It wouldn't be hard to track them down. I needed to do something to make my anger go away before taking it out on the wrong person. Why was this so hard? I'd never lost control like this. Ever.

A hand fell on my shoulder, and I removed

myself from Morgan's grip, keeping the loveseat between us.

"Please, give me a minute," I said, and she held up her hands.

She pushed her tongue against her cheek, the glimmer in her eyes saying she wanted to argue. "You need a drink?"

"A drink won't help this."

"How do you do it? Look different, I mean."

My fingers twitched, and her gaze shifted to my claws. "Glamour spell."

"Magic's real, too?" she exclaimed, then let out a heavy sigh. "Guess I shouldn't be surprised."

"You don't seem surprised at all."

"I have my reasons. How did you know?" she asked before I could get my own question in. "You showed up right when I was in trouble. Were you at the bar? I don't remember feeling you there."

At her words, my brow arched. "Feeling me?"

"You're not the only weird person on campus."

I wanted to ask her to explain, but another rush of heat coursed through me, and I gnashed my teeth. My hands trembled, and I glared out the windows. It was dark enough. I could make it out of here without being spotted. A trek through the woods might be a good idea.

"You didn't answer my question," she said.

"And I'm not going to. There's too much that you can't understand and that I can't tell you."

"Now, why don't I believe that?"

"I'm a demon, Morgan," I snapped, whirling around and pinning her with a glare. Her brow rose, and she crossed her arms, staring right back at me. "You have no idea what I'm capable of doing. I could hurt you, and I won't let that happen. I'm glad you're safe, but I need to go."

I stomped for the door, but she rushed to it first, pressing her back into it.

"Oh no. You're not going to pull that shit."

"I'm not in control," I whispered, biting off the words.

"I can help you."

"No," I yelled, and she didn't even flinch. "Just, no. I need to leave. Please."

"Will you slow down for five seconds? It's my fault you're like this, so let me help you."

"Your fault?" I thought of how those guys had her cornered and what they planned on doing to her. If I hadn't made it in time, if I didn't get the vision—I smashed my open palm against the door, imagining it as one of their heads I was crushing. Morgan's eyes never left mine. I leaned in, the comforting scent of falling leaves and cinnamon teasing my nose. "You did nothing wrong. If anything happened to you tonight," I cut myself off, shaking my head and sending my already ruffled hair flying.

"But nothing did." Morgan cupped my cheek, and I stilled at her touch. "I'll admit I don't fully understand what's going on right now or who you are, but I can feel you, Dagon. There's not one damned thing about you that's going to make me run the other direction."

A quiet growl vibrated through my chest. I pressed my other hand flat to the door beside her head. She simply held me, her gaze searching. My anger softened, and my bulging muscles relaxed. I went from thinking of her in the alley to how I held her in my arms last night. How she'd felt pressed against my body. This wasn't how I wanted to tell her who I was. She'd witnessed the ferocious demon, and I wished I could take those moments back. She licked her lips. My eyes darted to them, longing to kiss her. I lowered my head, ready to do just that until I spotted my shadow on the wall, horns and all, and immediately backed off.

No matter what Arkon or Cyrene told me, or what I saw in my visions, I was a demon. Giving in and allowing Morgan to be part of my life would only lead to danger.

"I have to go," I murmured.

This time, I picked her up, and set her aside. She protested, but there was too much at stake for her to be with me. Too much for us both to lose. The shadow-creature was still out there, as was the murderer. Maybe once they were taken care of, I'd let myself be with Morgan. Tonight told me one thing. I lost control far too quickly around her when she was in trouble. What would've happened if there'd been other students nearby? What if next time, I wasn't able to calm down at all?

Ensuring my glamour was in place, I grabbed the doorknob.

Morgan snagged the back of my flannel shirt and held on. "You're a liar then? Is that what you're telling me?"

"Morgan."

"No, you don't get to *Morgan* me." She tugged on my shirt, and I gave in, turning around. "You said you wanted to date me, remember? You said you wanted to try this, and so do I. You think I care what you are?" She pressed her hand where my heart was beating against my chest. "I know what you feel for me, and I'm not about to let you walk out that door thinking you have to stay away to keep me safe or whatever."

A flash of her covered in blood and screaming appeared in my mind. I opened the door, but she reached around me and shut it again. She flipped the lock and pressed her body into me, pinning me there.

"I want you." The weight behind those three words sent a different heat pulsing through my veins. "If you go, I'll follow. You can't hide from me."

The predator staring back at me from her light brown eyes set my blood on fire. I was used to seeing that look in the mirror, but to witness it on Morgan broke the last of my resolve. She'd hunt me down no matter where I went because she knew what I felt. There was no more trying to pretend she wasn't mine. How could I?

Insatiable hunger exploded inside me. I went to kiss her when she flattened her hands to my chest, pushing me back. "No glamour," she whispered. "I want the real you. All of you."

I hesitated, then let the spell fall. Her smile lit up her eyes. Lightly, she traced her fingers over my natural face, taking her time as if trying to memorize every detail of my jaws and cheeks, then higher to my forehead. She brushed her fingers through the silver and white hair around my horns. I cursed, gripping her hips. I grunted when her hands continued their exploration down my shoulders and arms all the way to my hands, holding her tight. My eyes closed, unsure how long I'd be able to stand this torturous pleasure she created. I peeked into her thoughts and growled at everything she wanted to do to me laid bare.

She gripped my short horns, and I crushed her to me, my eyes flying open and latching onto hers. They sucked me in, and there was no stopping the passionate madness that surrounded us. I captured her mouth with mine while she squeezed my horns, clinging to me like a lifeline. I grew lost in her touches and her lips moving so perfectly against mine. Skin, I needed to touch bare skin. My hands slipped under her shirt, and I pressed my palms to her back. They knew exactly where to go, guided by Morgan's body reacting to me, speaking to me. It wasn't so much her mind I read, but the very essence that made her who she was. I traced my fingers down her spine, and she trembled, winding her arms around my neck. It wasn't nearly enough, and we carefully stepped our way further into her apartment.

The backs of my legs hit the edge of the small

sofa, and I sank onto it, taking her with me. She straddled my lap as if this wasn't the first time we'd been so tangled up in each other's embrace. Remembering how much it had set her off last night, I moved my hands to her sides, feeling her up from her waist to the undersides of her breasts. She squirmed in my lap, and I groaned against her mouth, thrusting my tongue into its depths. A quiet moan was my reward, and I let my hands trace her ribs then lower to her hips. I barely dipped my fingers past the waistband of her jeans, then I dragged them back up, sweetly caressing the sides of those delicious mounds through the thin fabric of her bra. She pressed herself harder into my lap, and I bucked my hips, loving how her eyes became hooded with desire. I kissed along her jaw then down her neck, each little noise she made adding to my driving need to have her—every shift of her body bringing more of mine to life.

I tugged her shirt down, exposing the tops of her breasts. Hungrily, I pressed my face to them, kissing and licking until she was burying her hands in my hair. When her fingertips brushed past my horns, I barely kept my growling in check.

Too much. This was all too much. And at the same time, it wasn't nearly enough.

"We should, we should slow down," I whispered, pressing my lips to her neck.

"Do you want to stop?" she asked, shoving my flannel shirt over my shoulders.

"Fuck, no," I growled, and she laughed.

"Good. Neither do I."

She worked my flannel off and tossed it behind her. My t-shirt went next, and she gave me a wicked grin. Languidly, she kissed me while her fingers danced around my abs, then lower. She undid the button of my jeans but didn't go any further. She dragged her nails back up my chest, around my neck, then up into my hair. Her hips ground into me, and I lost any notion of stopping what we were doing. Morgan was mine, and I was going to have her tonight.

Reaching between us, I took hold of the V-neck of her shirt. The sound of fabric ripping was punctuated by her gasp of pleasure. She shed the ruined shirt exposing her chest graced with a black, knit bra. With one sharp claw, I tore through the fabric.

"You owe me a new bra," she said, her words breathy.

"Worth it."

Her chest heaving, I tucked my claws away and lazily relieved her of the bra, too. Two pert, pink nipples stared back at me. Her breasts fit perfectly in my palms. I brushed my fingers along the sides of her chest, and she dug her nails into my shoulders, squirming in my lap. Seeing her so aroused only set me off more. I lowered my head and sucked a nipple into my mouth. She gasped, pressing my head closer. I flattened my hand to her back, holding her to me. Her hands grabbed my horns, and I licked her nipple until she was cursing. I switched to her other one, begging for attention. Listening to her thoughts and her body, I had Morgan on the edge of ecstasy in seconds. My jeans threatened to tear from how swollen my cock was, but gods, she was beyond gorgeous losing herself in my arms.

It was going to be a long night. I ravished her mouth once again, deciding that tomorrow we might not see the world outside her front door.

7

MORGAN

Dagon's fingers expertly undid the button on my jeans and slid the zipper down. I was lost between my driving passion and his desire to bury himself inside me. Seeing his true form, hearing him say he was a demon probably should've terrified me.

It set me on fire with need instead, knowing this demon, this predator, was mine. And he was on the hunt. He wasn't the only one, though.

I scooted back on his lap enough so I could get my hand to his shaft, which I was desperate to feel. The continuous surge of energy coming from Dagon was like a caress. Every glide of his hand or his fingers, every press of his lips, and gentle graze of his teeth over my body was felt twice. I trembled, overwhelmed by him and needing more at the same time. He knew how to touch me to make my body call out to him. I lost focus of what I'd been trying to do, entranced by his hand slipping down my stomach and to my jeans. His fingers pushed through curls and barely brushed against my sex when he grunted and pulled back.

"Damned jeans," he muttered, and I chuckled. He stood me up, yanked my jeans and black panties down with one fierce tug, then lifted me right back onto his lap.

His palms smoothed up my thighs to my hips, then cupped my ass. I pressed my naked skin to his groin, gently riding his cock through the denim. A thrill of pleasure sent a jolt through me at the friction. He captured my hips and rubbed along my sex. It wasn't enough, and his hand was there the second I thought it. He massaged my clit, leaning me back so his hand could glide down my swollen and dripping wet cleft. He grunted when his fingers caressed my entrance but didn't fill me yet. I pouted, rolling my hips to urge him on. His hand glided up my stomach then between my breasts. Lovingly, he held my throat and thrust his tongue into my mouth. The embrace had me fumbling to touch every inch of him I could reach while he continued to drive me crazy with that damned hand of his.

How did he know what I wanted before I even did? I was right on the edge when he was back at my sex, his fingers teasing my sheath. They just slipped inside when he removed them again and felt me up, tracing each curve like it was his only reason for living. He licked a hot trail down my neck and sucked hard on my nipple until I threw my head back, face scrunching in pleasure. His fingers sought out my bead, driving me even closer to that glorious abyss of satisfaction. When he finally plunged his fingers within my depths, he thrust them hard and fast, pushing me over that ledge.

I groaned, shaking in his arms. He increased the pace, and I rode his hand until my limbs went limp, and I sagged against his chest. I tried to speak, but my mouth wasn't working right then. He picked me up and carried me to the bed shoved in the corner of my room. He tossed me onto it, and I laughed, bouncing on the mattress. Catching his hand, I pulled him down with me, eager to have him free of his last bit of clothing. Through our kissing and laughing, like we'd lost our minds, we managed to get his jeans and briefs off. His shaft bobbed into view, and I licked my lips, hungry to have him. I wrapped my hands around him. He plunged his tongue past my lips the same time he bucked his hips, thrusting into my hands. He was burning hot against my skin. My inner muscles clenched in anticipation of his rod filling me soon enough.

But I wanted to drive him crazy, first.

I pinned him to the bed, kissing him while my hands continued to lazily squeeze and glide along his shaft. He licked my lower lip, burying his hand in my hair, but I shimmied out of his hold and down the length of his body. I kissed my way across his chest, and down his abs, following the dusting of black hair leading to his cock. I swirled my tongue around the soft head, grinning when he shifted on the bed. I sucked just the tip of him into my mouth and his growl reverberated around the room. I pulled more of him in, pumping my hands down the rest of his length. Hearing him come apart urged me on. I kissed and sucked, licked and squeezed, his panting telling me he was close to falling over that edge himself.

I massaged his sack, and he bucked his hips. Hands grabbed my hips, and I gasped at the shock of ecstasy exploding within me. He'd lifted me up and swung my lower body around so he could torture me with his mouth. His tongue thrust into my sex, then licked my clit. When he sucked on the delicate bundle of nerves, I moaned around the cock swelling even more in my mouth. He pinned my hips to his chest, ravishing me until I was crying out, straining to get closer. I gave up on finishing him off, too lost in the tumultuous pleasure taking hold of me. He swung me back around again, then covered me with his body while tendrils of delight continued to shoot through me.

His kisses were tender. When his knee parted my legs, I gladly spread them wider for him. I glanced up, staring in awe at Dagon and the energy emanating from his body. I'd felt it, but now, I saw it clear as day. His eyes shimmered green, matching the hue coming from his horns glistening in the overhead light. A paler green surrounded him, then reached out for me, too. It connected with my body and seeped beneath my skin, far deeper than it had so far.

"Mine," he whispered roughly, then slanted his lips over mine.

He was everywhere at once, and I lifted my hips, needing him inside me. His hands shifted to the short black metal post headboard behind me. He gripped the upper bar and, staring into my eyes, moved his hips forward. His tip barely penetrated my sex, and I bit my lip, dragging my nails down his sides. He did it again, the shallow thrusts controlled and tearing me apart in the most beautiful ways. My head thrashed on the pillow until he said my name. My eyes latched onto his, that predator stare softening into something else entirely.

That look stole the heart I'd been more than ready to give to him.

His arms tensed, strained from keeping himself in control. Each gentle push within me built up the anticipation until I thought I was going to lose my mind. Holding my gaze, he thrust all the way in, and we groaned together. Feeling him stretch me set off the orgasm. Every glide in and out of his cock made it increase in pleasure almost unbearably more.

"Dagon," I gasped, lifting my hips.

He thrust forward again, filling me fuller than I ever thought possible. My hand inched toward my clit, but he beat me to it, rubbing it furiously while he continued to thrust home again and again. I wanted him to let go, sensing him holding back. He'd never do anything to hurt me or scare me. I tried to tell him that, but the words never made it past my lips.

His eyes glowed brightly, and he slipped free of my sheath. I groaned at the loss, then found myself on my stomach. He dragged my hips back into the cradle of his body, his cock rubbing along my soaking wet cleft. I sighed at him kissing my spine and cupping my breasts. He teased my nipples, and I buried my hands in the sheets. He pressed his shaft to my opening again, and I gasped at how slow he stretched me all over again. This time when he drew back, I sensed the last coils of control fall away. His energy collided with mine, and he buried himself inside me with a growl that vibrated all the way through me.

A spring of pleasure tightened in my belly until it came apart, leaving me dizzy and gasping for air. Dagon plunged in one final time, his body burning within and around me. We fell to the bed in a shaky heap. I shuddered the second he slipped free, then rolled over so I could face him.

He tucked my messy hair behind my ear and pulled me into his arms, kissing my forehead. I snuggled into his warmth, content to stay there the rest of the night. The energy remained, gliding over us in waves like we were lying on a beach, feeling the tide come in. Nothing else reached me while I was in Dagon's arms. I picked up on his worry amongst the growing sensation of love and perked up.

"Stop it."

"Didn't do anything," he said, but he avoided my gaze.

"You're worried. I'm not going anywhere," I promised, kissing the center of his chest. His arms tensed around me, and I kissed him again.

"Morgan," he whispered, and I grinned at the growl that came along with it.

"Hmm?" I kissed his collar bone, then up his neck. When I sucked on his earlobe, his hips jerked, and I felt his cock swelling once again. Curious, I glanced up to his horns. I grabbed hold, and his mouth was right back on mine while he pinned me to the bed.

"Playing with fire," he murmured against my lips.

"I always did like fire," I replied, then took control of the kiss, sucking on his tongue. He fumbled for the blankets, yanked them over our heads, and showed me how easy it was going to be to burn with him.

THE SMALL T-REX lamp on the nightstand was the only light in my apartment. Its glow was enough for me to make out the tattoo that covered Dagon's entire back. This one had some of the same strange letterings within it, much like the ones on his arms. I knelt beside him while he laid on his stomach, hugging my pillow. We'd been dozing off and on for the last hour, but now I was wide awake, my mind overflowing with questions.

I traced the intricate curling lines that formed three interwoven circles. The words followed the curves. There were smaller ones within them and what looked like vines and runes of some kind. Dagon's shoulders twitched, his lips curling.

"That tickles," he murmured sleepily.

"Why do I get the feeling this is for something?"

He opened one hazel eye and peered over his shoulder. "Protection ward. Keeps certain beings from finding me easily, amongst other things."

"So you tattooed them on your back?"

"Easier than having to remember to carry them on my person," he explained as if we weren't talking about magic and demons.

"Beings like what? Other demons? Hell, what else is real?"

He rolled to his side, giving me a lovely view of his naked body. His brow arched, but he didn't tackle me to the bed as I hoped he would. "We should probably talk at some point."

"How do you do that?"

"Do what?" he asked.

"That innocent smile doesn't work with me, hate to tell you."

He raised a brow. "Because you can feel me?"

I picked at imaginary fuzzies on the sheet wrapped around my body.

"Make you a deal. I'll answer your questions if you answer mine. Seems fair."

"What do you want to know?"

His eyes glimmered. "Everything, but I know you're about to explode over there, so you can ask first."

"What else are you?" I asked and cringed. "Sorry, that came out wrong."

"I know what you mean." His warm laughter washed over me, and he took hold of my hand. He trailed his fingers over my palm, following the various lines on my skin. "I can read minds, but I try not to. With you, it's harder to stay out."

"Why?"

His neck reddened, and he cleared his throat roughly. "I'm not sure."

"Does it have anything to do with why you said I was yours when those two guys came after me? And a little while ago?"

He rolled onto his back, eyes fixed on the ceiling.

The severe furrow in his brow was more than enough to tell me how much he wished we weren't having this conversation. His energy warmed and caressed me without him even realizing what he was doing. With it came a glimmer of anxiety, confusion, and the predator lurking just beneath the surface. The need to protect what was his.

I poked him in the ribs, and he scowled. "We made a deal, remember?"

"Demons aren't like humans," he whispered, dragging a hand down his face. I caught that hand and held it firmly between mine. "Our nature's a bit more intense."

"Kind of figured that part out, what with the snarling and the growling and all."

"It's not just that. We guard what's ours with a fury unlike anything else in this world. And you, you were mine the first night we met. I knew it deep in my bones, in my soul. I don't know how to explain it, but I can't live without you. You're mine now, and I'm helplessly yours." He sat up, his eyes darkening. "I'm sorry that I'm dragging you into something you might not understand. I don't have to stay—"

I dove into his arms, kissing him and pushing him right back to the bed. "I thought it was just me," I whispered, my lips on his.

"Not even close." The back of his hand moved against my cheek, and I spotted his claws extend just a hint. "This isn't too much for you?"

"I fell for you that same night. Demon or no demon, you're mine, too. Nothing will change that. Humans can be just as possessive."

His arms held me close, and we kissed, exploring each other's mouths until he sighed.

I frowned. "What?"

"You have more questions." He tapped my forehead, grinning. "It's distracting. Your thoughts are louder than usual tonight."

"Can you blame me? I have a demon in my bed." Reluctantly, I sat up and put a little space between us so I could focus. "Okay, so demons are real. Do you all read minds?"

"No. It's a rare gift, just as it is with humans." He sat up, too, resting his back to the wall.

"Is that how you knew I was in trouble?"

"Ah, no, that'd be something else. I get visions every now and then, too."

Visions and mind-reading. That I hadn't seen coming. Then again, I hadn't exactly seen the whole demons being real thing happen either, and here we were. I was so comfortable around Dagon. Touching him, kissing him. It was all perfectly natural to me. I honestly kept forgetting he had horns. Well, not entirely. I smiled, thinking of grabbing hold of them again. His answering growl told me he'd read my mind.

"Later," he promised. "Let's get through this conversation first."

"If you insist." I let the sheet fall, and Dagon growled my name, his eyes shimmering. I was never going to get tired of seeing that or hearing the beast that he was coming out. My beast. His growl deepened, and I laughed. This was going to be fun. "What else is real? Vampires? Werewolves?" I asked teasingly.

"Vampires usually keep to themselves. Most of them have modernized how they get blood. It keeps them from getting unwanted attention. Werewolves, shifters, whatever you want to call them—they're arrogant jackasses most of the time."

"You're serious?"

"I am. Witches are real, too."

I wracked my brain for what else could possibly exist. "Fairies?"

Dagon grunted. "Most of the fae are too bright and cheery for my liking. Depends on which kind of fae you're talking about, though. There's a lot of them. They tend to stay in their own pocket realm."

"Pocket realm? Do demons have one of those?"

"We do. It's what you'd call the Underworld, but it's not filled with the dead. Just demons."

"I feel like I should be taking notes."

He snagged my hand, giving it a gentle squeeze. "There's no hurry to learn about everything in one night. Trust me. It's not enough time."

"Why are you in college? Is that something all demons do? Decide to live with humans?"

His lips thinned, and the shimmering in his eyes went out. "That's a story for another night."

I thought about pushing the issue, but the energy in the room shifted. Grief and anger competed with each other until he shook his head. Whatever he wasn't telling me must have to do with why he had wards tattooed on his back and arms.

"Your turn," he said, and I hung my head. "You sense what I feel. What everyone feels?"

I wiggled my hand back and forth. "It's not the easiest thing to explain."

"I've got nowhere else to be." His energy embraced me even when he didn't physically move to do it. I shut my eyes, soaking in the sensation. He scooted closer, and I found myself sitting with my back to his chest and his arms, forming a comfortable hideaway from the rest of the world. His chin resting on my shoulder was the most normal thing in the world. I sank back into him, letting myself relax the rest of the way.

"I feel energy and emotions. Sometimes both. I thought I might be an empath, but I couldn't ever find anything about the energies. Like with you," I said, lifting my hand toward the subtle green haze in the air coming from Dagon. "I can see it."

"Like an aura?"

"I don't always see colors, though." I let my hand fall in frustration. "I feel it all the time. Energy pressing in around me. Sometimes it's good. Sometimes it makes me sick to my stomach. The emotions are the same way. It's why I hide in here a lot. People I've known for a while are easier for me to be around. I sort of get used to them. Then there's you."

I turned around in his arms, kneeling between his thighs. "I'm worse?"

"No. You stop it all from reaching me like a barrier of some kind. If I'm around you long enough, your energy lingers like I'm wearing a coat made of it," I said, grinning.

He gently held my chin, his thumb running over my bottom lip. I sucked it into my mouth, and his pupils dilated. "I've been protecting you all this time, and I didn't even know it."

"I guess you were. So, now you know I'm a freak of nature."

"Bit harsh when you're with a demon." His lips curled, and I gasped at the tingling sensation that encompassed my body, driven by a sudden rush of primal desire from Dagon. I shivered, my eyes closing. His claws tickled the sides of my breasts, followed by the tender skin underneath them. I inched closer, and he hauled me onto his lap, so I straddled him. "I don't think I'll ever stop wanting you," he whispered, kissing his way from one shoulder to the other.

"Good, because I'm not even close to being done with you yet."

The sheet got in the way. With an aggravated grunt, he yanked it free, tossed it away, and pressed his cock against my sheath. I sank over him, taking him in to the hilt and holding him within my depths. His head fell to my chest, and I leaned back, fumbling to find his horns while his mouth devoured my nipple and his hips softly ground against me. I grabbed hold of those hardened points, and he sucked harder, drawing a moan from my mouth. I was carried away by the waves of his energy and emotions. We had more to talk about, I knew that, but right then, Dagon's hands on my body were all I cared about. I picked up the pace, riding him hard. He held fast to my hips, staring deeply into my eyes while we inched closer to release. He kissed me, his tongue mirroring his shaft still thrusting within my trembling sex. I lost the rhythm, but he picked it right back up, laying me out beneath him.

"Mine," he growled against my neck. "Always be mine."

"Right back at you," I managed to reply before he pulled a sharp cry from me after adjusting the angle of his thrusts. I hadn't just fallen for Dagon. I'd toppled headfirst over a ledge I never wanted to come back from.

8

DAGON

I breathed in, and the scent of cinnamon met my nose. A lazy smile stretched across my lips, and I took another deep breath in, then let it out. Morgan. Last night came back to me in snippets of pleasure that hardened my already swollen shaft. It hadn't been a dream. Her soft moans filled my memory, and I stretched my arm out to the side, searching for her warm body.

Confused at finding nothing but bed, I sat up and opened my eyes.

The bed was empty, but my gaze immediately shifted to Morgan. She wore tight black yoga pants and a knit purple top without a bra on. She was doing yoga in the living room. Quietly, I moved to the edge of the bed, admiring her curves each time she stretched into a new pose. Her eyes were closed, but the twitch of her lips was a dead giveaway she knew I was awake and watching. She moved into another position, holding her arms out to her sides while she bent one leg into a side lunge. She leaned into the stretch, and I rose from the bed, stalking toward her.

Her chest rose and fell more quickly the closer I came. I stood behind her, my hands hovering over her bare shoulders then down her arms. I moved lower, drifting over her sides and hips. She nibbled her lip, her steady form faltering.

"Dagon," she breathed, and I nuzzled her neck. She came out of the stretch, leaning into me.

"Morning." A small part of me was worried that last night and right now were all a dream. Yet, Morgan never disappeared from my arms, and the room didn't fade away. This was very real, and I wasn't going to waste a second of time with her.

I sought out her soft mounds, growling when her hardened nipples pressed into my palms. I wanted to draw the moment out and make her squirm. A quick peek inside her thoughts and all notions of taking it slow were gone. Her scent enveloped me, igniting the primal urge to have her. My hands roamed over her body, easily tearing through her clothing as if they were made of paper. She chuckled, reaching her arm around to latch onto my neck. I pinned her to my body with one arm while my free hand sought out her sex. I slipped a finger within her, cursing to find her so warm and wet just waiting for me. I dragged my fingers back out, palming her then massaging her clit. She shoved her ass into the cradle of my hips, turning her head to kiss me. I obliged her, plundering her mouth with my tongue while my fingers twisted inside her until her knees wobbled.

She told me without words what she wanted. I guided her to the bed, spun her around, and laid her out before me. Seeing her spread her legs wide to accommodate me made my cock painfully hard. She gripped it in her hands, pumping the length hard and fast. Growling, I shoved her hands away, grabbed hold of her hips, and thrust in all the way. She cried out, her inner muscles clenching me each time I shifted forward. I lifted her hips, and her curse turned into a sharp cry that probably woke her neighbors. The notion of what was happening hit me at that moment. She wasn't just feeling her pleasure. Oh no, she was feeling mine, too.

Giving her a wicked grin, I focused solely on what she did to me.

Her reaction was instant. She yanked me onto the bed with her, pinned me down, and straddled my body. She impaled herself on my shaft, then leaned back. I massaged her clit, and she pressed her body into mine hard as she could. I rolled us over, never leaving her, and finished us off with a few frenzied thrusts. I buried my face in her neck, groaning my release. I fell to her side, struggling to catch my breath and unable to stop smiling.

"You," she mumbled, poking me in the chest. "That's cheating, you know."

"I have no idea what you mean."

"Liar." She slid her legs against mine until they were tangled together. I found her hand and brought it to my lips. "We have class in an hour."

"Says who? You look like you might be sick. Probably gave me the bug. We should stay in."

Her laughter warmed me, and I bundled her into my arms, kissing the top of her head. "You know we shouldn't miss it. But I'm free in between and all tonight."

She shook her head. "Only a bookworm would want to go to class today."

"If I don't make myself leave this bed right now, then I won't for the rest of the week."

She kissed my chin, and I glanced down to see

her bright eyes brimming with love I'd seen in my vision of us together. Knowing what followed, I turned away, willing my anxiety over her safety to stay hidden. Morgan didn't need to know how worried I was about that future not coming true.

"What's wrong?"

Damn it. Why did she have to be so sensitive to me? "It's nothing."

"You're not still worried about this, are you?" She lightly ran her fingers down one of my horns.

I growled, hugging her. "You're gonna have to not do that in public."

"It's fascinating." She did it again, and I pinned her to the bed once more, easily spreading her legs with my knee. "Dagon."

"I warned you."

I kissed her neck and her shoulders, then lower. My lips brushed against the sides of her breasts, and she shuddered. Her ribs were sensitive, too, and I treated them to the same slow ministrations. When she was breathless, I eased up her body and barely filled her sex with my shaft. Her eyes lightened, and she dragged her nails down my back. The shallow thrusts drove me about insane as they did her, and gods were they worth it. The first tremor rocketed through her and into me. I thrust all the way in and her back arched. Having her in my arms chased away the fear those horrifying visions brought.

I'd hoped to convince her that staying in bed all day was a great plan, but twenty minutes later, we were stepping out of the shower, despite my best efforts to keep her in there longer.

"You're ruining all my fun."

She patted my cheek then kissed it. "Stop your pouting. Just have to make it through a few classes, then we can pick up where we left off." She hesitated, then shook her head.

I chanced a look at her thoughts and held her hand. "I'm not worried about us."

"Just checking. Wish you didn't have to hide who you are."

"Been doing it for years. It's better than the alternative."

"I don't know. Watching a bunch of college students screaming while running across campus could be pretty entertaining."

At the door, I lifted her off her feet in one more hug to get us both through the morning. I grinned at the sight of her lips, red from our kiss, then silently cast the spell for my glamour. She ran her hands through my hair, chortling when I growled at how close she was to my horns.

"Nice to know that still works even when you don't look all demon-y."

"Demon-y, huh?"

"Yep, you heard me." She picked up her tote, slung it on her shoulder but didn't open the door. "Crazy. Yesterday, I had no idea so much could exist in this world. Now, I don't know, my life feels more manageable. Feels like it should be the opposite. Does that make sense?"

"As long as it makes sense to you, I don't care."

"You should've asked me out sooner," she murmured over her shoulder. "Just saying."

"I had my reasons," I whispered too quietly for her to hear, then followed her out the door. She locked it behind her, and we walked hand in hand through her building out to the commons. She stood on her toes to kiss me, said she'd see me in class, and walked away. I had to swing by my rooms for a fresh change of clothes and started that direction.

The apartment was empty, thankfully, and I ducked into my room to change. I gathered my books for the day, placed them in my leather messenger bag, and was at the door ready to leave—

A sharp pain exploded behind my eyes.

The last few hours spent with Morgan disappeared, and I fell into a nightmarish scene. She was covered in blood once again, sprinting across a gravel road while something massive howled and rushed toward her.

By the time it ended, I was on the floor, clutching my hands to my head. Whatever was coming after Morgan was getting closer. This time, its clawed hand nearly snatched her into the shadows. I clambered to my feet, needing to keep Morgan by my side. We were definitely going to be spending every night together. She wasn't about to be out of my sight unless she was in class.

Whatever monster was after her, I doubted it'd attack in the middle of an anthropology lecture.

Gods, least I hoped whoever controlled it wasn't that mad. We'd be entering into a whole world of hurt none of us would be ready for.

FRIDAY BROUGHT torrential rains and thunderstorms that caused the power to flicker in and out all day long. I stared out from under the overhang, searching the commons for Morgan. I'd tried to talk her into skipping her last class for the evening. It was turning out to be one of her rough days. She hadn't looked too great when I left her at the doorway to the lecture hall two hours ago.

I squinted through the heavy downpour and finally spotted a familiar violet fleece jacket and matching tote bag. She was walking with her friend Kayla. I grunted. I wasn't sure what that woman's problem was with me, but all she did was glare anytime I was around. I'd spoken to her maybe twice in all the time I'd known Morgan. I was fine with simply ignoring her until it became an issue with Morgan. She'd already apologized for her friend's weird behavior. I told her it wasn't a big deal and not to worry about it. As long as Morgan was happy with us being together, I couldn't give two shits what Kayla thought.

Morgan's shoulders were hunched, and her hair, which had been in a clip earlier was down and looked like she'd been running her hands through it nonstop. It was a habit I noticed we both had. I sighed. Her day had appeared to have gotten worse in the last couple of hours. I darted into the deluge, keeping my head down to keep the rain out of my eyes. By the time I jogged to the other side of the commons, Kayla was gone.

Morgan gripped the strap of her tote bag so hard

her knuckles paled. Her eyes were closed, and from the tense set of her jaw, her teeth were clenched.

I quickly took hold of her hand and pulled her into a tight embrace. She pressed her face into my wet flannel shirt, let out a heavy breath, then looked up.

"Hey."

"You don't look so good." I hugged her until she smiled and stood on her toes to kiss me.

"Long day. More than ready for it to be over."

"Over as in you want tonight by yourself or over as in beer, movie, and pizza at my place? I think Zane said something about Mack coming over tonight, too. If you're up for it."

She threw her head back with a groan. "You know we're never going to hear the end of this."

Somehow all week, we'd managed to dodge Zane and Mack. They weren't stupid. I was sure by now they'd figured out what was going on since Morgan and I weren't exactly trying to hide our relationship. That, and I'd spent every night since Monday at her place.

"We don't have to," I started to say, but she shook her head.

"Nah, it'll be good for us. Just going to be hard not to blab everything."

"Not sure they're ready to hear the whole truth yet."

I hesitated, but I'd waited too long to let her know about Cyrene. If I didn't bring it up, I sensed the witch herself would show up on campus. I'd been reluctant to talk to Morgan about meeting Cyrene. Realizing and accepting I was a demon was enough craziness for one week. After seeing her today, I knew Cyrene was right. If Morgan didn't find a way to deal with the emotions and energies that came from being around people, she'd end up a lot worse off than she already was. She'd turn into a full-blown hermit. I couldn't let that happen.

"I've been meaning to tell you, there's someone I know who might be able to help you with your situation," I said.

"Really? Who?"

"A witch. Her name's Cyrene. I think you should meet her."

"Sounds like a good time. Why do you not feel happy about this?"

"She's a bit much." And I had no doubts Cyrene would gladly tell Morgan everything I had yet to tell to her about. Such as the visions I'd had of us together, her death, and being chased across a gravel road covered in blood. Oh, yeah, Morgan meeting

Cyrene was going to be awesome. "I'll call my brother, see if we can't pop out on Sunday for a visit."

"I finally get to meet your brother?"

"Yeah. I have two, actually. Arkon's the middle one, and you'll like Jasmine. She's his girlfriend," I said, then frowned. Morgan would probably get along really well with Jasmine and Cyrene. The more I thought about it, the more I wasn't sure her meeting them at the same time was a good idea. The three of them in the same room would be nothing but trouble. I peered into Morgan's thoughts. The turmoil she struggled to hide from me was all too easy to read. I was out of options if I wanted to ease her daily discomfort before it became unbearable. "Sunday, then?"

"Sunday will be perfect."

With my arm draped around her shoulders and hers at my waist, we meandered around campus, sticking to the overhangs as much as possible. When we had to finally leave the safety of the buildings, I shrugged out of my flannel and gave it to Morgan to hold over her head. She laughed, said it was just rain, and took off into the storm. She stomped through puddles soaking her jeans and getting me wet in the process. Thunder rumbled, and lightning streaked across the sky, creating rivers of electric blue light in the black thunderheads. We made it to my building and inside. Zane and Mack weren't back yet, so I tugged Morgan through the apartment to my room.

"You're soaked," I said, laughing. She shook out her dripping hair, beaming at me from beneath the tangled locks. "Feel better?"

"With you, always."

"Should've gone to your place to grab you some clothes." I rummaged through the chest of drawers, pulling out a black t-shirt and some gym shorts that'd probably fit her if she cinched them at the waist. "You could change into these and dry... dry off." I swallowed back a groan. How had I not heard her clothes hit the damned floor? "Think that's a record."

She grinned, running her hands up her naked sides. "You want to stand there talking about my putting on clothes, or you know, enjoy the bit of time we have before the others get here."

The garments fell from my hand, and she was in my arms a heartbeat later. She shoved at my sopping wet shirt, giggling at the struggle it was to get me undressed. I kept my lips to hers as much as possible, fumbling and maneuvering our way across the bedroom to the bed. My glamour fell, and she imme-diately reached for my horns. I couldn't get enough of her after that, but she was due some payback for what she did to me this morning.

I might be able to read minds, but she was getting too damned good at knowing exactly how to set me off. She'd done it this morning, leaving no time for me to return the favor before we had to go. I slipped down her body, spread her legs, and buried my face between her thighs. Her hand smashed into the bed, the other pressing into the back of my head. Words fell from her lips, but they made absolutely no sense. I thrust my tongue into her depths then sucked on her clit. Her legs fell open wider, and I relished in the ecstasy already taking hold of her body. I didn't let up until she was quivering in my grasp, her inner muscles throbbing around the fingers I filled her with to find that one spot to send her over the edge.

I moved up the bed, covering her with my body. She was so damned wet, I slid right home after adjusting my hips. Her nails dug into my hips, and her right leg wrapped around my waist while I buried myself over and over within her.

A door opened and slammed.

Zane called out.

I smothered a laugh, burying my face in Morgan's neck. Not once did I slow down. I moved faster instead, racing to get her to climax all over again. She clapped her hand over her mouth, attempting to quiet her moan that rose in pitch. I lost the rhythm from our combined laughter. She shuddered beneath me, torn between amusement and pleasure.

"Dagon? You back yet?" Zane called through the door.

Morgan shook her head, eyes wide. She still had her hands over her mouth, but the skin around her eyes crinkled. She was grinning under those hands.

"Yeah, I'll be out in a second," I yelled back.

"You know if Morgan's swinging by tonight?"

I thrust hard and deep. Morgan's eyes fluttered shut, and a quiet moan escaped her.

"Think so," I replied, and she smacked my arm. My brow arched, and I pulled out, teasing her with the shallow thrusts that drove her wild.

"Sweet. It should be a fun night," Zane replied.

His footsteps retreated, and the next thing I knew, Morgan had rolled us over and pinned me to the bed. I cupped her breasts, then pinched her nipples at the same time. She cursed, covering her mouth again, and shaking with laughter. I bucked my hips, and her eyes rolled back. The orgasm rico-cheted visibly through her and right into me. I grabbed her hips, thrusting upward one final time, my release making me go cross-eyed for a second. She collapsed onto my chest, silently laughing.

"You didn't expect me to stop, did you?" I asked when she sat up, nailing me with a scowl that turned into another smile.

"No, guess not."

I kissed her nose and her cheeks, then her neck. "We should probably get out there."

She slid to the side, her cheeks red, and I took my time admiring her gloriously naked body. I noted the skull and bones studs in her right ear today. "What are you staring at?"

"An incredible woman," I replied sweetly, leaning in to kiss her.

Ten minutes later, we finally made it out of my bed, cleaned up in the bathroom thankfully attached to my room, and exited the bedroom with my glamour in place. Zane stood at the breakfast bar, Mack on the other side of it. They froze when I walked over, Morgan at my side. Her hand was securely held in mine.

"What movie is everyone in the mood for tonight?" I asked.

Zane's gaze slipped from me to Morgan, then to our hands. He laughed, holding out his hand to Mack. "You lose. Pay up, man."

Mack rolled his eyes but reached into his back pocket and pulled out his wallet. He handed over a twenty, shaking his head at Morgan. "What were you two betting on?" she demanded while I struggled not to laugh.

"Whether you were in there or not. And here I thought you were the decent one out of us."

Morgan stalked around the breakfast bar, playfully punching Mack in the shoulder. He ended up putting her in a headlock and messing up her hair until she pinched his arm, and he let her go. They shoved and poked each other, bantering and laughing. We carried beers and pizza to the living room, picked out a horror movie series to watch, and settled in for a relaxing evening together. I'd been worried that being around her brother with me in the room would be awkward for Morgan. She sat down on the couch beside me, put her feet in my lap, and snuggled close without even batting an eye. Mack couldn't stop grinning. He gave me a thumb's up at one point, and Morgan lobbed a hunk of pizza crust at his head.

For those few hours, we were normal. I wasn't a

demon, and I almost couldn't tell she was an empath who could read energies. We laughed and jumped, cursed, and threw pizza crust at the TV when the bad guys came on the screen. I couldn't remember the last time I had this much ridiculous fun. Four movies later, Morgan was passed out on the couch, snoring quietly. I scooped her up, and after nodding a goodnight to Mack and Zane—both quietly catcalling while I shook my head—I carried her to bed.

I tucked her in beneath the covers and held her close. My eyes closed, and I was out in seconds.

When I jerked awake, the room was pitch black. Morgan was beside me, clutching a pillow to her and sound asleep. Shrugging off whatever had awakened me, I lay down to get back to the dreams I'd been enjoying. A sharp pain burst behind my eyes. I gasped, struggling to get out of bed before I could awaken Morgan.

"Dagon? What's wrong? Migraine?" Her hand landed on my shoulder.

I tried to speak, but all that came out was a snarl. The woods appeared in my mind's eye, then a woman. She was running, tripping over roots of trees, and screaming for help. A massive creature charged through the forest after her. She spun around at the last second, a blue orb of light in her hands, and let it fly. The creature shrieked but didn't slow down. The woman's dying scream echoed in my ears while the rest of the horrid images faded away.

"The woods," I whispered, "have to get to the woods."

"What are you talking about? It's the middle of the night," Morgan pointed out. "Dagon, slow down."

I was already on my feet, flipping on the lamp and fumbling for clothes. "You don't understand."

"About your migraines?" Her brow shot up the longer she stared at me. "Shit. Those aren't migraines, are they."

"Not exactly."

"What did you see?"

I tugged a t-shirt on over my head and finished buttoning my jeans. "Doesn't matter. I just need you to stay here, alright? Stay inside, stay safe, and wait for me to come back."

"Yeah, not happening." She threw the blankets back and went to grab the clothes we'd hung up in the bathroom to dry.

"You're not coming with me."

"The hell I'm not." She came out of the bathroom dressed in record time, dragging her hair back into a messy bun. "Whatever you saw was clearly bad, and it's making you go all demon-y right now. Tell me what it is, and I'll consider not tagging along to make sure you don't get yourself in trouble."

"I'm a demon. I can handle myself."

She planted her hands on her hips, her naturally arched brow arching even more. "Cocky much? Demon or not, I can feel the anger and the nervousness you've got going on."

Gritting my teeth, I threw my head back with a grunt. "It has to do with the murders."

"You saw someone getting killed?" she exclaimed, and I shushed her, glancing at the bedroom door. "Seriously? How many times has that happened?"

"Every time."

"Wait, if you see it, then shit! We might be able to stop it." She rushed past me to the door and was out in the main hall before I caught up with her.

"Are you insane?" I snapped.

"Do you think you can go out there alone to catch this maniac?" she challenged. "Demon or not, it's better if you have someone to watch your back. We going or what?"

I snagged her hand and pulled her down the hall

with me. "We're going to have a serious discussion later about how you seem so eager to throw yourself into the hellmouth of danger that may or may not lead to your death."

"Bit overdramatic, aren't we?"

"Not even close."

"Might want to put your glamour up. Could be students out."

I stopped at the top of the steps. I hadn't even realized it wasn't cast. Morgan was going to be far more trouble in my life than I was ready for. With my glamour in place, we set off again, telling Morgan she was to do everything I said and no arguing, or I'd drag her back to the apartment and lock her in my bedroom. She agreed, squeezing my hand. It still amazed me how she was taking everything about this new world in stride. She found out demons were real and was with one. Didn't slow her down. Found out I could read minds and had visions. Also did nothing to stop her in her tracks.

I even finally told her why I was pretending to be a college student. Why I was on the surface at all. Talking about my parents' murders had been harder than I expected after all this time. She'd held my hand the entire time and simply sat with me. Her only comment had been that she was technically dating royalty. I wasn't sure why, but that had made me laugh. It'd been the emotional release I'd needed without even knowing it.

My instincts about Morgan not being an ordinary woman were spot on.

I wasn't so sure if I was excited by that fact or terrified.

Visions of her replayed in my mind. I growled, shook my head, and tucked them away. We had a chance to save this other witch. That's what I needed to focus on right now.

At the edge of the woods, I sniffed the air. Another storm was on the way. The breeze had died, and the leaves on the trees had gone utterly still. The witch had been running out of the clearing with the dead tree. We'd start there and work our way out. Not letting go of Morgan's hand, we entered the woods, me keeping her right behind me. She hardly made a sound. Not even when she walked right into a spider web. The severe focus in her light brown eyes was like she was a predator on a hunt.

Like she was a damned demon herself. That was the second time I'd seen that look, and I was more than curious about what caused it. I'd have to ask her later how she managed that.

The dead clearing appeared through the thick-trunked trees. I stopped, putting a finger to my lips. Morgan nodded, and we eased our way out of the woods, stepping onto the dead grass. There were no body parts scattered around this time, and I stopped trying to block Morgan's view once I saw there was nothing here except more black candle nubs, scattered herbs, and eggshells. I took out my cell and snapped a few pictures, wincing each time the flash went off.

Morgan tapped my arm, but she wasn't looking at me. Her wide eyes peered into the woods to the north of the dead tree. "Feels wrong somehow," she whispered. "Something's there."

Something, not someone. Mentally cursing myself for letting her come, we stalked in the direction she'd pointed. We barely made it a yard or so in, before Morgan's grip on my hand turned painful.

I glanced over my shoulder, brow furrowed. She shook her head, squeezing my hand even harder. Needing to know what she sensed, I slipped into her mind and growled. The bitter tang left in my mouth, followed by the sensation of a hand crawling up my spine, told me what was in these woods with us tonight. Evil.

Sticks cracked to our right, and I spun, keeping myself between whatever was out here and Morgan.

A shadow separated from the trees, looming in the distance. The stench of rotting meat, blood, and magic clogged my nose. The figure was taller than me and had one horn jutting out from the right side of its head. The other one appeared to be a broken stub. Red eyes flared.

I bared my fangs, my claws extending to their full-length, ready to fight it off.

Those eyes, those were the same damned eyes from my vision of Morgan.

I growled. The creature lumbered forward, then whipped its head around as if listening to something else. It snorted and took off into the forest, crashing into trees as it went. The sound died away after a few moments. I stayed where I was, ensuring it hadn't tried to circle back around to surprise us. The scent of it was gone, too, and when I heard nothing for another thirty seconds, I eased forward.

We made it to where the creature had stood, and I grabbed Morgan's shoulders, forcing her to a stop. "It's not coming back. I want you to stay right here by this tree."

"Why?"

"Just do it, please."

She gulped. "There's a body, isn't there. How do you know?"

"I can smell it," I grunted. "And demons can see fairly well in the dark. Stay here."

Leaving Morgan by a tree, I pushed through the short shrubs and thorns pricking at my skin through my jeans. I didn't need light to see the body had been torn to pieces, just like the previous ones. The rancid smell of death hung in the air. I held my breath, sifting through the shredded clothing and hunks of flesh, searching for any clue as to who this woman was. From the vision, she was obviously a witch, one strong enough to cast elemental magic. A glint of silver caught my eye, and I knelt, avoiding the puddles of blood the best I could.

"Damn." I lifted the chain, eyeing the amulet hanging from it. This one was of a pentagram with several sigils along the edge of the round charm.

"Dagon?"

"Yeah, I'm coming back." I hurried to Morgan and took her hand. "We need to get to campus. I'll make an anonymous call so the cops find her."

"This isn't the first body you've found."

It wasn't a question, so I didn't answer, guiding her through the trees and away from the grisly murder scene.

"That's why you freaked out on me the other night. That night, they said they found another one."

She socked me in the shoulder. "You moron! Are you trying to get yourself killed?"

"What am I supposed to do? Ignore what I see?" I snarled, hanging my head. No matter what I was shown, I was always too late to save them. Did that mean I'd be too late to save Morgan when that monster finally came after her? It had the same red eyes, but this didn't appear to be made of shadows. "Besides, I'm not its target."

"How do you know that?"

"I just do."

"You're so full of shit. You can't know that." She shivered, and I pulled her into my arms, resting my chin atop her head. "What was that thing? I know you said a lot of shit exists, but that, I wouldn't even know what to call that."

"I don't know, but I know someone who might have answers. Good thing we're going to my brother's house Sunday."

"The witch?"

"Yeah. If she doesn't have an idea of what's killing people out here, I'm not sure who will. If we don't stop this monster, though, more witches are going to die."

She leaned back, smoothing her fingers over my forehead. "I'm sorry."

"For what?"

"For you seeing so much death. Can't be easy."

I scowled down at her, not that she could probably see my expression in the dark. "It's not, but it's my burden to bear, not yours."

"Dagon—" s

I cut her off with a quick kiss. "We need to get back to campus."

On our way to my apartment, I put in an anonymous tip to the cops. A light rain started to fall, and we walked quickly through the commons then inside. Back in my room, with Morgan tucked safely in my arms, I asked her about what I'd seen in the woods. The way she'd been so focused.

"Sometimes I can use the energy around me, tap into it somehow. I might've been channeling you," she explained, her fingers tracing the lines of my tattoo perfectly as if she could sense the power in it. "I don't try to do it, but I figured not being scared shitless was a good idea."

"Probably, but next time, you're not going with me."

"You're not going out there by yourself," she argued hotly. I found myself flattened to the bed a second later, the fierce look right back in her eyes while she held me down. "Promise me, Dagon. You're not going after that monster by yourself."

I cupped her face and sat up to kiss her. "I promise." I kissed her again, and soon we were shedding our clothes, our hands starting a frantic dance of caressing each other's bodies. When I filled her that night, it was about far more than simply giving her pleasure.

It was a promise that no matter what came next, I'd do whatever it took to keep her safe.

9

DAGON

"You're going to have to let this go eventually," I murmured, gripping the steering wheel harder.

"How about you stop poking around in my head?" Morgan shot back.

"Hard not to when you have that pinched look on your face."

She crossed her arms and glared out the windshield. "Are we there yet?"

I pulled off the main two-lane blacktop road, and the tires crunched over gravel. The drive leading to Jasmine and Arkon's farmhouse was long and winding, taking us through a patch of dense woods surrounding the property. The last day and a half had been stressful. I'd come clean about having visions involving the murders since they started. Morgan had freaked out that I could've easily gotten myself killed on any of those nights.

I'd hoped to leave the conversation at that, but Morgan asked if there was anything else she didn't know. That was a loaded question, and I did my best to avoid answering it without making it sound like I was lying. She might not be able to read minds, but she called me out for holding back the truth all the same.

I parked in the pull-off outside the farmhouse and turned the Tahoe off. "I don't like fighting."

"Who said we're fighting?"

I laughed. "Really? What do you call this?"

"This is me being annoyed at you for thinking I can't handle whatever it is you haven't told me. I know you said there was a lot you couldn't tell me yet, but I think we're past that point. Don't you? Or do you not trust me?"

I took hold of her hand and pulled her toward me as much as I could with the center console in the way. I kissed her, burying my free hand in her hair and loving how she melted into my touch. "It's not about trust," I said against her lips. "I'm not ready for you to know everything. That's all."

She pressed her lips to mine then sat back. "Okay."

"That's it?"

"I don't like that you're keeping secrets from me, but if you're really not ready to let me know, then okay." She fiddled with the zipper on her purple fleece jacket. "I was worried, I guess."

"About what?"

"We've only been officially dating a week, and it feels like we skipped right through the fun first few months of being together phase right into whatever craziness this is." She tugged on her dinosaur studs and avoided my eye. "That and you're already dealing with so much, then I come along, and I've got this weird energy reading thing. I know how much you worry about me. What if I'm a distraction? I could be the reason that monster out there hurts you."

I shoved the console out of the way and pulled her over to me. I hugged her the best I could in the front seat of the SUV. "I waited too damned long to tell you how I felt. I'm not about to suddenly put our relationship aside because shit's hard right now. And honestly, it feels like we've been together more than a week."

"Same," she whispered, squeezing me back.

"Whatever you're hiding from me, you'd tell me if it was bad, right? If it was going to put you in more danger or something? I might not be a demon, but I can help keep you safe, too."

I kissed the top of her head, locking down my emotions the best I could. "I would."

She leaned back and studied my face. After a few seconds, she smiled and scooted back to her seat. "We should probably get inside. This is going to be fun," she added, sounding worried.

"Arkon and Jasmine will like you."

"And the witch?"

"I have a feeling she's going to adore you."

I knocked once we climbed up the porch steps.

Jasmine yanked open the storm door, then pushed open the screen, beckoning us inside. "You must be Morgan," she said, then pulled her into a hug.

Morgan grinned at me over Jasmine's shoulder. "That'd be me. Thanks for having me over."

"Are you crazy? You can come over any time. Finally, someone else I can talk to about what it's like being with a demon." Jasmine let go of Morgan and hugged me, too. "Dagon. Nice to see you looking so much better."

"Better?" Morgan asked.

"It's nothing," I said, giving Jasmine a warning look.

"You know that shit doesn't work on me. I have to deal with your brother's annoyed glares, remember?" Jasmine's hands fell to her stomach. I followed the movement, confused.

"Uh, how far along did Cyrene say you were?" I asked.

"You're pregnant?" Morgan asked with a grin. "That's so exciting!"

"It is," Jasmine agreed, then turned to me. "And apparently, this pregnancy is not going to be normal. She thinks I'm only going to carry the baby for six months. I'm already halfway there."

The bump that hadn't been there the last time I saw Jasmine was undoubtedly there now. I couldn't recall any other human who'd become pregnant by a demon. Arkon was probably losing his mind right now.

"Arkon's in the workshop," Jasmine informed me. "Cyrene should be here soon. Can you go tell him for me? I'll take good care of Morgan for you." She beamed at me, and I growled.

Morgan stood on her toes and kissed my cheek. "We'll be fine. Gives us a chance to chat."

"That's what I'm worried about." I gave Jasmine

one last pleading look not to stay too much and went out through the kitchen door to find Arkon. I followed the sounds of hammering to the workshop. "This place is certainly coming along."

Arkon smiled, put another nail into the two-by-four he was attaching to the new wall, and turned around. "Almost finished."

"You going to work on the nursery next?"

Arkon's eyes shimmered, and he tossed the hammer onto the makeshift workbench he'd built. "I was expecting seven more months at least. Now, shit, I've got three, maybe? I'm going to have a baby."

"Yeah, you are. You two will be just fine."

"What if we're not?" he whispered, glancing worriedly toward the farmhouse. "I'm not exactly the nicest demon around."

"It's your kid. You'll be alright."

He grunted in reply, opened the blue cooler nearby, and pulled out two bottles of wheat beer. "Gods, I hope so." He handed me a beer, a silly grin spreading across his face. For the first time in years, Arkon was genuinely happy. I took a quick gander into his thoughts and hopped right back out, clearing my throat. "I felt that."

"Sorry. Didn't expect to fall into that."

He chuckled, clapping me on the shoulder.

"What can I say? Pregnancy makes her hormones all over the place. That woman's going to wear me out."

"Sounds dreadful," I teased.

"Morgan with you, I assume?" he asked, and we left the workshop.

"Yeah. Jasmine said Cyrene should be here soon, too." I stopped him short of the back door, the sounds of Morgan's and Jasmine's laughter filtering out the open kitchen window. "She doesn't know anything about the visions I've had of her, and I want to keep it that way. Don't bring it up tonight."

Arkon's lips thinned. "You have to tell her."

"Why? So she can have something else to worry about? No. She doesn't get to know. Bad enough she found out I've been trying to hunt down this killer."

"You said it had horns?"

"More like antlers, really. One antler. The other had been broken off. And the creature reeked of death. Morgan thought the energy around it was, well, evil."

The beer bottle in Arkon's hand shattered.

"I'm sorry. I shouldn't have gotten you or Jasmine involved. We can go, meet Cyrene somewhere else."

"No. You're right to come to us. We're family."

"And? I don't want anything happening to Jasmine or the baby."

"It won't," he snarled, his claws and fangs growing while the muscles in his shoulders bunched. He cursed and got control of himself. "My protective instincts are overkill right now. I don't want you out there hunting down this thing alone, either. Besides, from what you said, it sounds as if it's going after witches in Wellsville. Thankfully, we're a couple of hours away, and Jasmine isn't a witch."

"No, but Morgan might be," I whispered, finally admitting the truth aloud. After speaking to her and learning how sensitive she was, it made sense. And if she was a witch, that red-eyed behemoth would be coming for her. I squinted into the woods. They seemed so peaceful now in the middle of the day. I sensed nothing ominous out there waiting to attack. We were safe here. Cyrene had this place so heavily warded mosquitos didn't even get through.

"Let's get inside." Arkon nudged me along. "We'll get this mess sorted one way or another. You could be wrong. There are humans with gifts who aren't witches."

"Dagon!"

Morgan's panicked shout came from the kitchen, and Arkon sprinted to the house, with me right behind him. We entered the kitchen and found Morgan holding Jasmine's hands while she gasped for air. Her eyes were wide but glazed over. Arkon quickly took hold of her, wrapping his arms firmly around her body while he whispered in her ear.

Morgan shook her head, whispering an apology, but I told her it was nothing she did.

"We were just talking, and then she couldn't breathe," Morgan whispered, her eyes glued to Arkon who was holding Jasmine. She tilted her head, her brow wrinkling. "His aura It's surrounding her."

"She gets panic attacks," I explained. "Caused by a demon when she was a teenager."

"That explains the fear. It appeared so suddenly." Morgan's hand slipped into mine. I held it until Jasmine finally slumped in Arkon's arms. She assured him she was alright, and he turned her around, kissing her forehead.

"Sorry about that," Jasmine said to Morgan with a smile after Arkon guided her to a chair.

"Been a while since you've had an attack." Arkon smoothed her hair behind her ears, his other hand resting on her pregnant belly. "Are you sure you're alright?"

"I'm awesome." She dragged him closer by his shirt and kissed him. "Stop the growling. We have company, remember?"

Arkon lifted his head, turning to Morgan. He held out his hand to her, and she took it. "Nice to meet you, Morgan. I'm Arkon." His gaze flicked to me. "At least Dagon can stop moping around now."

"He was moping?"

I glowered at my brother, who winked back at me. I didn't get a chance to respond because a gust of wind rushed through the house, bringing with it a storm of brightly colored red, orange, and green leaves. Arkon muttered a curse, and Jasmine smacked his arm. The leaves fell away, revealing Cyrene. She wore shades of green and violet. She was barefoot, and her violet hair was decorated with glistening green and silver vines. Her dress was made of various layers of flowing silk held together by two copper and silver clasps shaped like owls at her shoulders. She looked more like a fairy today than a witch.

Cyrene's violet eyes glowed, turning to me. "I'll take that as a compliment."

"Wait, can she read minds too?" Morgan asked, her eyes wide in awe while she stared at Cyrene. "Oh, that was probably rude. I'm sorry. I'm uh, I'm Morgan. Nelson. Morgan Nelson." A nervous laugh escaped her lips. "Sorry. I have no idea what's going on with me."

"It's the magic, dear," Cyrene explained with a kind smile. She tilted her head, tip-toeing through the mess of leaves on the kitchen floor until she reached Morgan. "You are certainly special. My, my, where have you been hiding, my darling little witch?"

"What?" Morgan shook her head. "I'm not a witch. Am I?"

I exchanged a look with Arkon. Cyrene just confirmed my greatest fear. If Morgan was a witch, the stakes just got a whole lot higher. Who was to say the next time that monster attacked, it wouldn't go after her? I'd already seen her being chased across a gravel road. There were several in and around the woods by campus. I didn't understand why that event never came to pass. Not that I wanted it to, but was I really seeing that far into the future? The furthest I'd seen was a couple of weeks at most. Though that didn't count the visions I had of Morgan and me together or the shadow looming up to snatch her away from me. My temples throbbed, and I drained my beer, wishing it was something stronger.

"You have some magic in your veins," Cyrene told Morgan, circling her. She lifted a lock of her hair and let it fall. "Hmm, interesting. Very interesting."

"What is?" I asked with a growl.

"Oh, calm down, Dagon. I'm only getting started. Let me find answers for you both before you start threatening me."

"It's not going to hurt or anything, is it?" Morgan asked.

"No, child, not one bit. I do want to hear everything about your family, though. Let's start with the basics. Why don't you demons make yourselves useful and get everyone a drink? Maybe something to snack on? It's going to be an awfully long afternoon."

My lip twitched, but Morgan gave me a smile. She wasn't worried, and I tried my best not to be. That turned out to be impossible, knowing what I feared all along was probably going to come true.

And I might be helpless to stop it. I might be helpless to save her.

"You doing okay?"

Morgan leaned on the front porch railing, her chin resting on her folded arms. "I'm fantastic."

I stood beside her, unsure if she wanted me here or not right then. She straightened, leaning into my side, and I draped my arm around her shoulders.

"Could be worse things to learn."

"Aside from the fact that I'm an energy witch? Yeah, probably." She wound her arms around my waist, hugging me. I gave her what comfort I could, willing myself not to let her pick up how I was also not doing okay with this latest bombshell of news. "If my aunt hadn't been killed, she probably would've been able to tell me all of this. Instead, I spent my entire life thinking I was a freak of nature."

"I mean, you're still a freak," I teased, and she groaned. "You're not alone. You know that, right?"

"I do. A small part of me wishes I didn't have this ability or magic in me. Make life a lot easier."

"Do you really not want it? Cyrene's a powerful witch. I'm sure there's a way she could take it from you. Bind it somehow," I said.

Morgan's brow furrowed while she studied me. "You'd be okay if I did that?"

"It's your life. I'll be in it no matter if you have magic in your veins or not." I tucked the hair that had fallen behind her ears and tilted her chin up so I could kiss her. "But I think you'd regret it."

"Regret being miserable every day?"

"If you give yourself a chance to understand it, have Cyrene teach you, you'll be able to make it a true part of you." I shrugged, kissing her again. "But that's merely my opinion. You decide what you want to do, and I'll be here for you."

"Even if it means I'm getting dragged further into the world of magic and monsters?"

"You let me worry about the monsters."

"Yeah, that's not going to happen. What if I can figure out how to make all this energy shit useful? I could help you."

I growled, scowling down at her. "No."

"Man, Jasmine was right. Demons are way over-protective of what's theirs."

"I knew you two getting along would be bad."

Morgan chuckled, then dragged me down to her level. She captured my mouth in a heated kiss that had me wondering if it was time to head back to campus. Jasmine told us we could stay the night, but I wasn't exactly keen on having my brother in the room next door from Morgan and me. Especially not after what I saw was on her mind once we were alone.

"What were you and Arkon talking about?" she asked.

I'd hoped she wouldn't ask. While Cyrene had

been walking Morgan through what she was and how her abilities worked, Arkon and I had stepped outside to talk about the murders more. He'd said he'd call Calrod with the update and to give me some backup on campus now that Morgan was most likely going to be a target for this monster. He hadn't heard of anything like it either. We needed to speak to Cyrene about the murders, but she was checking on Jasmine and the baby first.

"Making a plan," I finally replied.

"And do I get to know what this plan is?"

"I'm not sure yet," I admitted, fiddling with a lock of her hair. "Whatever that creature is, the people it's murdered are not humans."

"What are they?" she asked.

I kept playing with her hair, unable to look away and unwilling to say it aloud.

Her eyes narrowed, and she shifted on her feet. Then she let out a very quiet, "Oh, shit."

"I don't want you getting any more involved. I can handle it."

"And if you can't?"

"Please don't argue with me."

"Why the hell not?" she snapped, pushing her way out of my arms. "So this thing might come after me next? That sucks, but if you think for one damned second I'm going to sit back and play the damsel in distress, you're wrong. Whether you want to admit it or not, I can help, and that's what I'm going to do."

"You're not ready. You don't even know how to control your magic."

"That's why I'm going to learn. Don't go after it by yourself," she begged, gripping my shirt and hauling me to her. "I need you, got that? I need you alive, and it's not just because you ease the chaos around me. I need you because life is weird without you in it. It's colorless and dull, and I don't want that anymore. I want you, so don't you dare do something stupid, Dagon. I'll kick your ass if you do."

I growled, lifting her off her feet so I could kiss her until we were both breathless. She didn't know about my visions, which meant she couldn't even begin to understand the fear I was keeping locked away.

"I won't do anything stupid," I promised. "But that means you can't either."

"Deal."

The front door squeaked open, and Cyrene joined us on the front porch, her eyes glowing. "Who would've thought the brothers from the Underworld would be such charmers with the ladies?" She motioned for Morgan to come to her. She opened her hand, and a silver chain fell from it. From it hung a rune, the metal shimmering with green and blue light. "Wear this when you're not around Dagon. It'll help keep your abilities in check until you're able to come and train with me this summer."

Morgan took the necklace, admiring the pendant. "Thank you, really. I'm not even sure what I can do to repay you for this."

"You, my dear, simply need to promise to come to me and learn. All of you are keeping an old witch feel young again. And don't worry, in three months or so, someone else will be joining you." Cyrene's gaze skipped to me before it jumped to Jasmine and Arkon, who were stepping out the front door.

"What do you mean?" I asked. "I can't use magic."

"Never said you, Dagon, now did I?" Cyrene beamed at Jasmine.

"Wait, what?" Jasmine said with a nervous laugh. "I'm not a witch."

"Ha! Truly, you lot have given me so much entertainment lately. Of course, you're a witch, dear. How else do you think you're able to carry a demon's child?"

Jasmine's jaw dropped. Arkon growled, wrapping a protective arm around her.

"I'm off. I'll be seeing you soon, Morgan. And Dagon? You keep an eye out for that creature of yours. I'll see what I can find out. Do not go after it without speaking to me first. No point risking your life until we know what is and how to stop it."

Morgan gave me a bright smile, and I rolled my eyes. "I won't," I told Cyrene.

She waved, sauntered off the front porch, and whipped up a gust of wind and swirling leaves. When the last leave fell, Cyrene was gone, and the four of us were left standing in strained silence on the porch.

"I'm not a witch," Jasmine repeated. "I would've known, right?"

Arkon's brow rose. "Actually, I was wondering how you were able to get pregnant. And you survived being attacked by a demon all those years ago. I didn't want to say anything but—shit! What was that for?"

Jasmine punched him in the gut again, lot of good it did. "You're such a twat! Why didn't you say something sooner?"

"When was I supposed to tell you?"

"Any time would've been great," she argued.

"I was trying not to throw anymore at you. We've got a lot going on right now, remember?" He rested his hand on her pregnant belly, and Jasmine's shoulders slumped. She covered his hand with hers.

Morgan moved closer to me, smiling, no doubt at the love pouring from Arkon and Jasmine. "I'm sorry I didn't tell you, but I've been panicking over bounty hunters showing up, and being a father, and worried that it's all happening too fast."

Jasmine pulled Arkon down to her level and kissed him. I turned away. Morgan stifled a chuckle.

"It's not too fast," Jasmine assured him. "I'm terrified too most days, but then I remember I've got you and the fear goes away. You're mine, and I'm yours. Nothing's ever going to change that."

I turned back in time to see Arkon nip her lip and growl.

"Right, we'll just head out then." I guided Morgan to the porch steps.

"You don't have to go," Jasmine said, but she wasn't looking at us.

"It's alright. I'm not sure the two of you are going to be up for having house guests much longer." I held out my hand, and Morgan took it. "I'll call you if anything changes."

Arkon grunted in reply, already backing toward the front door with Jasmine in his arms.

"I like them," Morgan said when we were near the Tahoe. "Jasmine's a lot of fun."

"You should see her when she's drunk and not pregnant ," I said. Keys in hand, I opened the driver's side door. For some reason, my body didn't listen to me and climb into the vehicle.

"Dagon?"

I tried to speak, but a stabbing pain in my eyes cut me off. I sank to the gravel, the keys falling from my hand. Morgan ran around, grabbing hold of my shoulders to keep me upright. She yelled for Arkon. I fumbled for her hand, wincing when images exploded in my mind. The creature was running through the woods. There was no one around. No one screamed. I wasn't sure what I was seeing until it ran right into an invisible barrier. Violet sparks shot into the air. It roared, attacking the barrier over and over until finally, a crack formed. It howled in triumph and charged forward—

"It's here," I gasped, the vision ending. "It's here."

"What's here?" Arkon growled, helping me to my feet. "Dagon, talk to me. What do you mean?"

A furious roar echoed from the woods, sending birds taking off into the sky.

"Get inside," Arkon ordered Jasmine, his claws extending to their full length. His fangs did the same, and he snarled when the creature roared again. "Now, Jasmine."

"Go with her," I told Morgan.

She started to argue until I yanked her into my embrace and kissed her fiercely. Arkon did the same to Jasmine, and we waited for them to go.

"You both better come back alive," Jasmine warned. "Arkon."

"I know," he whispered. "Now go."

Morgan didn't say anything, but she didn't have to. I nodded, assuring her I'd come back, too. She and Jasmine took off for the farmhouse. The door slammed shut, and I turned my attention toward the woods.

"You said you didn't know what it was," Arkon murmured.

"It almost looked like a demon, but it was all wrong."

"Think it can bleed?" His muscles strained in his neck, and his shoulders bulged with his growing anger.

"I say we find out."

The invisible barrier surrounding the farmhouse sparked violet, lighting up the surrounding woods.

We braced our feet in the gravel, each hit to the barrier making my pulse race faster. I moved my foot again. The gravel crunched beneath my boot. Shit. This was a gravel road. The vision of Morgan covered in blood shot through my mind. It wasn't going to come true. It couldn't. Sharp cracks hovered in the air from the damage the warding had taken after the beast crashed into it over and over. Another hit and the magic shattered. The creature howled and charged forward. Trees groaned, being shoved out of the way of the monster. It lumbered closer, a hulking shadow emerging from the forest.

It couldn't get past us, not for anything. I snarled, Arkon bellowing a challenge beside me. The creature broke the tree line. I had a second to notice how messed up it appeared, then it sprinted forward, ready to kill.

"This is my fault," I snapped, staring out the front windows. "I never should've come here. All I did was put you in danger. And the baby! Jasmine, I'm so sorry."

"You didn't know it'd track you this far. Hell, you didn't even know you were a witch until today. Shut up and stop panicking."

My lips clamped at her bluntness.

"Besides, apparently, you're not the only witch," she reminded me, sighing. She took hold of my hand, giving me an encouraging smile. "They'll be okay. Arkon's not one to go down easy. Neither is Dagon."

"Don't they have another brother?"

"Texted him, but he hasn't responded yet. Reception sucks here." Jasmine hummed quietly under her breath. The song was horribly off-key, but it seemed to calm her down. "They're going to be fine. They have to be fine." Her panic and fear radiated off her and straight into me.

I gritted my teeth, working to control how much I felt. It didn't help I was too busy panicking myself. Watching Dagon and Arkon stand out there ready for an attack was a harsh reality I hadn't expected to deal with so soon. The creature roared, and it was like someone set off violet fireworks in the woods. We jumped at the loud crack.

"What was that?"

"The warding," Jasmine whispered. "It broke the warding."

I'd only known Cyrene for a few hours, but the power coming off her was palpable. If it broke through her warding, this creature was a lot stronger than Arkon and Dagon had imagined. A massive shape emerged from the trees. Jasmine and I were at the window, eyes wide and staring. The same evil energy I'd experienced the other night struck me in the gut, and I gasped, fighting not to be sick.

"That's the creature?" Jasmine uttered. "What the hell is it?"

"I don't know."

The beast stood at least eight feet tall. Its hulking form almost gave it the appearance of an extremely tall demon, but the horns weren't like Dagon's. The one horn that was intact was long and jutted out from the side of its head. It had smaller ones curling off it in jagged twists. The other main horn had been broken off, leaving a nub behind. Black claws extended from its fingertips, much longer than Dagon's. Fangs hung over its bottom lip, but its mouth wasn't normal. Its whole body felt wrong somehow, like it'd been twisted into this new shape by force.

Its massive jaws opened far wider than was natural, and it threw itself forward. I expected it to aim straight for the house. Instead, it threw Arkon to the side with one swipe of its arm and went straight for Dagon.

Dagon's fury kicked in, and he ducked under the first attack, then barely dodged the second swipe of those wickedly long claws.

He slashed his hand down the monster's face. Blood spurted from the wounds, but it didn't go down. Dagon went in for a second attack. A fist caught him in the gut, and the creature grabbed him by his hair, yanking his head back.

I yelled in a panic, but Arkon charged in, burying

his claws in the monster's neck. It released Dagon, and they tag-teamed it, rushing in to cut it, then leaping back to avoid being struck. Only a couple of minutes had passed, but the fight seemed to stretch on for an eternity. The longer I watched, the more I noticed that no matter what blows Arkon dealt it, the creature only had eyes for Dagon.

"Why isn't it going down?" Jasmine wrung her hands.

The beast sported numerous deep gashes and was drenched in blood. It should've weakened, but it never faltered. Arkon rushed in again to attack. The creature snagged him by the neck, lifting him off his feet. It roared in his face then tossed him into the side of the Tahoe. Arkon slumped to the gravel, unmoving.

"No," Jasmine breathed.

Dagon bellowed, enraged, and went after the beast. He nailed it twice in the gut and raised his hand to slash down its chest, but the beast caught his hand and twisted. Dagon's face screwed up in pain, and I yelled.

Jasmine took off deeper into the house, yanked open a closet door, and pulled out a shotgun. I sprinted to her side, and she handed me a second one and a box of shells. Dagon's pain and anger flowed right to me as if he were subconsciously reaching out, desperate to feel me one more time. He wasn't going to die. I wasn't going to watch that thing kill him. With the shotgun loaded, I raced to the front door. The creature had Dagon by the throat, his jaws wide as if he was ready to tear into him with his fangs.

"Stay here," I told Jasmine. I didn't give her a chance to argue and charged out the front door.

I was glad Mack and my dad had taught me how to shoot, I braced the shotgun against my shoulder and rested my finger on the trigger.

"Hey, asshole," I shouted.

The creature lifted his head, snarling at me.

"Run," Dagon rasped. "Get out of here!"

Ignoring Dagon, I watched the beast, waiting for a clean shot. It turned, holding Dagon to its side. With its chest in plain view, I squeezed the trigger. The shotgun slammed into my shoulder, but I'd struck the beast. It howled, staggering back and losing its grip on Dagon. I pumped the gun and shot it a second time, not letting it recover. Dagon was yelling, but the beast was in a frenzy. It nailed Dagon in the face with its hoofed foot, and he collapsed.

I shot it a third time, willing it to fall. Its eyes glowed red, and I cursed, fumbling in my pocket for more shells. I reloaded, my fingers shaking. The beast stalked toward the house, the same house where Jasmine was, behind me. I had to get it away from her and the baby. I stomped down the porch steps and shifted to the left, drawing it away from anyone else.

With the gun reloaded, I raised it to my shoulder again and fired. Its right shoulder jerked back. It lowered its head, and I thought it was finally going to fall. Then it lunged forward, and I yelped, barely managing to get off another shot before it snagged the end of the gun and wrenched it from my hands. It kicked me in the gut. I fell to my knees, holding my stomach and fighting to get air back in my lungs. It raised its hand, ready to strike, but hesitated. Its entire body trembled as if it fought against its nature to kill me.

Another shot rang out, and the beast whirled around with a roar. Jasmine stood on the porch steps, aiming her gun at its head. "Get away from her, you bastard!"

"No," I tried to yell, but it came out as a grunt.

The creature stomped toward Jasmine. She fired again and again, and then the gun clicked empty. She hurried to reload, but the beast took off at a run. Yelling furiously and tapping into Dagon's energy like I had the night in the woods, I threw myself after the monster. Power surged through my limbs, aiding me to move faster. Jasmine stumbled back, tripping on the steps. She fell, and it towered over her, ready to kill her. Just as those claws came down, I dove between them. Burning pain exploded in my chest, and I was thrown clear across the gravel drive.

"Morgan!" Dagon shouted, then he and Arkon were back on the creature.

I rolled onto my back, staring blankly at the sky. Streaks of pinks and reds chased away the bright blue it had been earlier. Something warm oozed across my chest, but I was too tired to comprehend what it was. A gust of wind erupted nearby, and I marveled at the beautiful array of leaves falling around me like rain.

A bright explosion of violet light blinded me. A woman's voice called out in a language I didn't understand but somehow spoke to me all the same. The beast howled one more time. The sounds of something large crashing through the woods came from behind me. Was it over?

"Morgan." Dagon's face came into view, his eyes shimmering bright green and his hands hovering over my chest. "Shit, I told you to stay in the house."

"I'm fine, really. Just a scratch."

He growled, pressing his hand down. I shrieked, and his lips thinned.

"Okay, maybe more than a scratch," I muttered.

"We have to slow the bleeding." He let out a stream of words in a rough language. I assumed they were all curses.

Arkon was yelling from somewhere nearby, and Jasmine was shouting back, defending our decision to jump into the fray. From the anger I felt pouring out of Dagon, I could tell he was barely stopping himself from scolding me. Whatever. I saved his life and Arkon's.

"Such a mess you all make." Cyrene knelt at my other side, sighing. "They'll heal easily enough. She's in no danger of dying, Dagon."

"See?" I said, and his lip lifted, revealing his fangs. "Whatever. Yell at me later."

"I plan to."

"Let's get inside, and I can patch you all up," Cyrene said, clicking her tongue. "I leave you alone for five minutes, and look what happens."

Dagon started to pick me up when he cursed, his face paling.

"What's wrong?"

"I'm fine," he told me and hoisted me into his arms. I flinched, the wounds on my chest protesting, but I didn't ask for him to put me down. I'd never seen him so furious or seen his energy pulse such a deep shade of green. Oh, he was pissed alright, and he wasn't the only one. Arkon was still arguing with Jasmine as they followed us into the house.

Dagon placed me on the couch then stood behind it, holding his right hand against his chest. He was covered in cuts and slashes, too. After ensuring Jasmine was unharmed, Cyrene came toward me. I wanted Dagon to be looked after next, but Cyrene ignored me and went to work on my wounds. I wasn't sure exactly what she planned on doing. I watched in fascination when several glowing vines slid down her arm and wrapped gently around my torso. Calming energy flowed from her to me, and I sank into the couch cushions. Once the bleeding stopped, she pulled a small glass jar from thin air and applied a dark green paste to the wounds, explaining in an undertone that it would speed up the healing.

"I don't see what the problem is," Jasmine snapped, and I turned my head to see her and Arkon standing nose to nose in front of the fireplace.

"You're insane," Arkon shouted. "That's the problem. That's always the problem. First, it was challenging a demon with a bat. Then it was threatening to ax murder another one. Now it's charging at an unknown monster with a damned shotgun? What were you thinking?"

"I was thinking of keeping your ungrateful ass alive."

"You can't simply run into fights like that."

"Don't." Jasmine jabbed her finger into his chest, glaring up at him. "Don't you dare tell me what I can't do. I'm not going to stand by and watch you die. How do you expect me to go on if I lose you, huh? How? We're having a baby, and I refuse to raise it without you."

"And I refuse to let either of you leave me," Arkon replied, gripping her shoulders. "I can't watch you die again. I won't do it."

Jasmine threw herself into his arms, and he hugged her, kissing the top of her head while they mumbled apologies and kissed.

"Don't go thinking this gets you off the hook," Dagon whispered.

"For what? Protecting you?"

Cyrene had moved away from me and was checking over Dagon's wounds. She held his right hand in hers. There was a bright flash of light and the sickening sound of bones being forced back into alignment. Dagon grunted, never looking away from me. Cyrene used the same healing magic on his hand, then quickly checked over the rest of his wounds. The vines spread, covering his body.

"You're lucky none of these are any deeper," she said.

"The creature was targeting him," I said.

Dagon scowled.

Cyrene frowned "What do you mean?"

"It didn't seem to give two shits for Arkon aside from getting him out of the way. It never came after Jasmine or me. Not until we started shooting it. And even then, it hesitated. It could've killed me, but it didn't."

"I am curious as to how it found you this far from Wellsville." The vines retreated into Cyrene's hand, and she waved it over my body, then Dagon's body. When she neared his pocket, she stilled. "Hand it over."

Dagon reached into his pocket and pulled out the necklace he'd brought from the latest murder victim. Cyrene took it, her eyes narrowing.

"A tracking spell buried beneath layers of shielding magic. Clever, very clever," Cyrene murmured. "It would appear whoever is committing these murders knows you're onto them and would like to kill you before it returns to murdering witches."

"I brought it here?" Dagon looked to Arkon, shaking his head. "I'm sorry. I had no idea."

"I won't say I'm not furious," Arkon said, still holding Jasmine securely in his arms, "but after seeing that monster, you're not going to fight it alone. You can't. I'd prefer if it didn't come back here, though."

"It won't," Cyrene assured him. "I'll redo the warding, make it stronger. As for you two," she gestured to Dagon and me, "expect a package from me tomorrow. It'll have items for you to bless both of your apartments to ensure the beast can't reach you there. There'll be protective charms as well. Keep them on or near you at all times."

"We have to stop this person," Dagon said.

Cyrene went to Arkon and healed his wounds, too. "We will." Her energy pulsed with concern, and her gaze latched onto mine. I sensed she was trying to tell me something, but I wasn't sure what it could be. Once Arkon was healed, she headed for the door. On her way there, she leaned in and whispered to Dagon. He blanched, growling at her back after she'd turned to go. She said she'd take care of the warding and be in touch.

The front door slammed shut, and a heavy silence fell over the farmhouse. I sat up, amazed at how quickly my wounds were healing, thanks to Cyrene. There wasn't any pain or discomfort. I sensed Dagon's eyes on me, but he never got a chance to speak. Arkon was across the room and hugging me the second I made it to my feet.

"Thank you," he said. "Nice to know you can shoot."

"Yeah, I learned young," I said, hoping to lighten the mood. "Can't believe I made it there in time."

"How did you?" Jasmine asked. "You were so far away, and then you were there."

"I might've tapped into Dagon's energy," I admitted. "Gave me a boost."

Growling came from behind me, and Dagon's anger was joined by his chaotic energy. The predator was alive and well within it, including the driving urge to protect what was his. He'd nearly failed, and it was tearing him apart.

"We should get back," I said. "Don't want to stick around any longer. I'm sorry for all of this."

"Don't be," Jasmine said, hugging me, too. "We're family. No one fights alone, not anymore." Arkon took hold of her hand and kissed the back of it.

I zipped up my fleece jacket to hide my torn shirt

and turned around. Dagon's jaw was clenched, and his lip twitched while he studied me. I said I'd wait for him by the Tahoe and stepped outside. The evening air was anything but refreshing. The energy of the creature still lingered. My stomach churned, and I quickly walked to the SUV, and climbed inside.

So much for today being relaxing and straight-forward. I'd hoped for a nice peaceful night after everything I learned. Too bad that wasn't going to happen. I slumped in the seat, knowing at some point Dagon was going to have to tell me how angry he really was. Nothing like an argument to end the weekend.

THE RIDE back to Wellsville was filled with Dagon's growls and my failed attempts to start random conversations. By the time he parked, and we were walking to my apartment that night, I was on edge because of how much he kept jumping from panic, to fear to anger, then on to another emotion. I unlocked my door and stepped inside.

I undid my jacket, checking out my ruined shirt. The salve had dried and came off with a simple brush of my fingers. Three red lines remained, scars to mark my new life. Nothing like baptism by fire to prove things were about to get even more exciting.

"Don't do that," Dagon snapped.

"Do what?" I asked, then realized he'd read my thoughts. "I'm okay."

He hadn't moved away from the door, though he'd dropped his glamour. His hazel eyes darkened, and his entire body trembled. "You think that's all I care about? That you're fine this time? You nearly got yourself killed. You understand that. You could've died tonight."

"But I didn't. What did you expect me to do? Watch that monster kill you?"

"I wasn't going to die."

"That's not what it looked like to me."

"You don't get it," he yelled, then swiped a hand down his face, his eyes wild. "I saw the attack happening. Saw it weeks ago, and there was nothing I could do to stop it. Nothing."

"Why didn't you tell me?"

He swallowed hard. "Why do you think?" His emotions cut off sharply.

I recoiled from the hollowness left behind.

"I can't do this," he whispered, and the pain that

came along with that short sentence stabbed me right in the heart. "I won't."

I pressed my palm to my chest, my heart shattering. "What are you saying?"

"Until this beast is killed, I can't be around you. I won't put you in even more danger."

"I'm going to be in danger either way. I'm a witch, remember?"

"The murderer is after me now. It's better this way. Once they're caught, once this is over, we can see where we're at."

"You're lying," I whispered. "You don't want to be with me."

"That's not what I said at all."

"Really? It sure as hell sounds like it to me. Whatever happened to not putting our feelings aside anymore, huh? What happened to that promise?"

"It's not that easy," he argued, his eyes flaring and his energy glowing right along with it.

"Then make it easy."

He backed toward the door. "I'm sorry."

"No, you don't get to run away from this." I rushed forward and grabbed his hand, stopping him from leaving. "I get that you're scared. I am, too, but this isn't the answer."

He hung his head, flattening his hand to the door. His claws dug into the wood, and he gritted his teeth. "Tonight was too close. Too damned close. I was wrong. All of it was wrong."

"I only did it to save your life."

"And I'm trying to save yours," he uttered, spinning around. "I've been trying since the night we met, but I can't do that if you're going to throw yourself at whatever monsters come your way."

I blinked, struggling to process what he said when it hit me. "You have been keeping something from me," I whispered. "You saw something else besides me getting hurt this evening. What is it?"

"Morgan," he pleaded, but I pushed him into the door.

"What did you see? Tell me, damn it."

"I saw you die," he blurted.

I flinched at the force of his agony slamming into me.

"I've seen you die over and over, and there's nothing I can do to save you. It's my fault you die, Morgan. Mine. I thought if I stayed away, it'd keep you safe, but the vision never changes. Now, though, now I think I just didn't go far enough. If I leave, it'll keep you alive."

I backed away, fumbling with the hem of my t-shirt. "I die? How?"

He hesitated, and I yelled at him to answer. "I don't know. There's a creature made of shadow, and it consumes you. I'm too late. I'm always too late."

"You've been seeing this vision the whole time?"

"Yes."

"But you don't know when it'll happen?"

"There's not enough detail, no," he said quietly. "Morgan."

I held up my hand, sensing he was still holding back. "What else did you see?"

He ran his hands through his hair with a curse. "I saw us together. We were laughing, and I felt," he started but shook his head.

"You felt what?" I pushed.

His eyes flicked to mine, and the wall he'd put up to block me out fell. The anger he'd been holding onto all night gave way for a storm of passion I wasn't ready for. I swayed on my feet, gasping at the love reaching out to hold me close even though Dagon wasn't physically touching me.

"And you want to throw that away?" I whispered.

"I want you to live."

"I can't do that if you're not with me." He couldn't feel my emotions, but he could read my thoughts. I reflected on every moment I'd spent in his arms. Every kiss and touch we shared. Every laugh and smile and quiet moment where we'd held each other close. I knew the second he slipped into my mind. His eyes fluttered closed, and he fell back against the door. "We belong together. You know that. Don't let fear win."

"Morgan," he growled.

"I don't care what you've seen. You're mine, and I'm not going to let you go that easily."

He pushed off the door, and I was in his embrace, his lips moving frantically against mine. I couldn't touch him fast enough, tearing at his shirt until he finally ripped it over his head for me. I flattened my hands on his bare skin. His heart pounded beneath my palms. I kissed down his neck then to his collar bone, nibbling in the one place that drove him mad. His rumbling growl echoed through and around me. His arousal pressed into my lower stomach, and I pressed my hips into his. I returned to his mouth, our tongues struggling for control of the kiss. Everything he felt, I did, too, and the rising tide of raw desire swept me away.

Dagon ripped my shirt the rest of the way off, and my bra was gone seconds later. Chest heaving, he drew back, his eyes narrowing on my chest.

Lightly, he trailed his fingers over the three long claw marks that ran from right above my breast to my collar bone. He lowered his head, kissing each one, and I buried my hand in his hair, pressing him closer. He nuzzled my chest, his short claws tickling my back. His touches went from frantic to tender, and tears burned in my eyes. He lifted his head, gently wiping away the few that fell. It'd been too close for both of us tonight. Too damned close.

He lifted me into his arms, carrying me through the apartment. When we reached the bed, I slid down his body. He captured my mouth all over again, his tongue flicking against my lower lip then plunging inside. We fumbled for each other's jeans, kicked the rest of our clothes aside, and tumbled into bed.

His mouth and hands were everywhere. The pulse of his energy added another erotic layer to every move he made. He palmed my sex, and I gasped at the burst of pleasure that one simple touch caused. He left far too soon and trailed kisses down my sternum to my stomach. The scruff on his cheeks sent enjoyable little bursts of excitement through me when he rubbed his face against my inner thigh. My legs fell open, and he took me with his mouth. I cursed, my back arching off the bed while he held my hips captive in his grip. His tongue teased my sex then he sucked hard on my clit. I longed to have him in my grip, but he stayed out of reach. My release came fast, and I shuddered, roiling in the ecstasy coursing through my veins.

He covered me with his body and kissed me. How he tasted of me only turned me on more. I dragged him closer, lifting my hips until I felt his cock between my thighs. I wrapped my right leg around his waist. His hand massaged its way down my thigh to my hip. I needed him right then more than I'd needed air to breathe. How could he have ever thought we'd be okay apart? His hips glided against mine, and I sighed at how he stretched me so completely.

"I'm never letting you go," he rasped, thrusting forward. "You hear me? Never."

"Good," I gasped. The pleasure built, and I bit my lip, the coil tightening impossibly more in my core. "Dagon."

He shifted from deep thrusts to quick, shallow ones that left me panting. I reached up, managing to grab hold of his horns. He lost control then and buried himself inside me with a fury over and over until we were both groaning and clinging to each other while our bodies quivered. He rested his forehead to mine, staring deeply into my eyes. I cupped his face, rising up to kiss him. He rolled us over, never leaving my body, and held me there. I didn't think either of us was ready to go again, but he swelled within my depths.

I moved slowly, drawing out the moment. He felt me up, and a rush of heat shot down my spine. My inner muscles clenched him, and he groaned, bucking his hips. I did it again, loving how his eyes brightened until they were glowing. He traced my ribs, his touch feather-light as it moved higher to my chest. His thumbs caressed my hardened nipples. He sat up suddenly, capturing one in his mouth and sucking. I fell back over his arm, which had been keeping me upright. His tongue swirled around the sensitive nub, and I squeezed his shoulders, a quiet moan falling from my lips. He growled my name, and our gazes locked. It was impossible to look away. He held my hips steady, and we moved like one person, coming apart at the seams only to be stitched back together. My cry was sharp, but I never closed my eyes. He shimmered with his release, his shaft growing rigid within me until he slipped free with a curse.

Somehow, he got us beneath the blankets and pulled them up over our heads. I curled into the heat of his body, falling asleep with his hands rubbing my back and him planting a kiss on my forehead.

When I woke with the sun, I was tucked protectively in Dagon's arms. I shifted, and he growled in his sleep, tightening his hold around me. I chuckled, shimmying up his body to kiss him. His cock hardened immediately against my thigh. Grinning, I rolled him to his back. His eyes fluttered open, and I rubbed my sex along his shaft. He growled, lifted me up, and filled me in one go.

"I could get used to this," I murmured.

He squeezed my ass, and I rode him, laughing at how incredible being with Dagon made me feel. He massaged my clit, and I came a few seconds later. He pulled out long enough to roll me to my stomach, dragged my hips back, and filled me again. One hand cupped my breast, tugging playfully at my nipple while his other held my hips steady. He sagged to the side moments later, and I grinned right along with him.

"Not a bad way to wake up," he agreed, his words breathy. He held my hand, our legs twining around each other's.

I kissed him then sat up, needing to use the bathroom. When I was halfway across the room after taking care of business, a box appeared out of thin air and fell at my feet. I yelped, jumping back. "The hell is that?"

"Cyrene."

"Right. Guess I assumed when she said package it'd be delivered the normal way."

"Sorry, lover, but you're not living in a normal world, not anymore." He scowled, clearly debating if he made the right decision last night.

"If you leave me, I'll hunt you down," I warned.

His eyes flared, and he growled. It wasn't just Dagon staring back at me then, but the predator that lurked beneath the skin. A fantasy of me running through the woods while he gave chase set off a spark of erotic images I couldn't stop picturing. Dagon had me back on the bed, giggling madly until he spread my legs and plunged inside. The quickie, fueled by my extremely horny imagination, set me on fire.

"We—uh, we should see what she sent," he murmured, his face buried at my neck.

"When I can move again." I tried to stand and sank right back to the bed. "Everything's wobbly. You know, we can't exactly give into fantasy when we're in public."

"Then I guess you should be careful what you

think," he warned with a growl. Languidly he kissed me, then pushed off the bed. He picked up the box and set it on the coffee table. "Looks like crystals for the warding of both our places." He removed eight white crystals that looked like quartz of some kind. "Spell to say with them. This powder we're supposed to sprinkle by the doors and windows," he said, holding up a large glass jar filled with a sparkling blue substance. "And these must be the protective charms." He set aside two small black leather pouches.

"Smells like cinnamon."

"Amongst other things." He sat back on the couch, running his hands through his hair.

Taking a blanket from the bed with me, I sauntered over and sat beside him. He draped his arm around my shoulders and drew me into his side. The coming days would be challenging, but we'd get through them together. I'd spend every one of them reminding Dagon why we were better together. We'd wasted enough time fighting our feelings. Now, I was going to embrace them head-on and whatever else came with them.

Dagon was my future.

Death would just have to wait a while for me.

11

"I can't believe the semester is almost over," I said, stretching on my way out of the classroom.

"You shouldn't be surprised this month went by so fast. You've been a bit preoccupied," Kayla said, not looking up from the paper in her hand. "At least we don't have to sit for a final in that class."

Her fake cheery tone was something I'd gotten used to hearing. It'd been a week since Dagon and I went to see Jasmine and Arkon. We performed the protection spells on both our apartments, and I made sure I carried my leather pouch at all times. The amulet Cyrene gave me to help keep my abilities under control was tucked beneath my shirt. If I wasn't around Dagon, this little guy did exactly as

Cyrene promised it would. I hadn't felt this good in so long. Well, unless I was with Dagon. If I could simply be with him all day long, we wouldn't have any troubles at all.

"I thought you'd be happy for me. Got a boyfriend and everything. Isn't that what you've been telling me to do for the last couple of years?" I mused while Kayla and I headed to the commons.

"Oh yeah, I'm thrilled."

I pulled her to a stop. "Alright, out with it. Is this just because I didn't go out with that Kevin guy?"

"You didn't even give him a chance."

"I did, but he just wasn't what I wanted. Why don't you like Dagon?"

"Maybe because he practically ignored you all those months, then suddenly, he's all over you? He's using you. How can you not see that?"

"Nice to know how much faith you have in me to make smart decisions about my own life."

Kayla sighed. "Look, I get that you think he's a good guy now, but he won't be forever."

"How would you know? You've never even talked to him. And he had his reasons for not being with me before. I just can't tell you them cause it's personal."

She barked a laugh. "Personal. Yeah, sure it is."

"What's your problem?"

"I'm looking out for you," she yelled.

Several passing students gave us weird glances. S

he pulled me off the sidewalk and into the grass, so we stood under an oak tree. "He's not a good guy. Can't you just trust me on this? He's nice now, but it won't last. It never does with guys like him. He'll use you, then he'll ruin you."

The venom in her words sounded like it came from someone else. She fiddled with the pendant on her necklace, glaring over my shoulder. I didn't have to turn to know Dagon had probably appeared and was looking for me.

"I'm sorry you feel that way, I am, but I'm with Dagon. Nothing's going to change that."

"You're making a mistake."

I shrugged. "Then it's my mistake to make. I'll see you around, okay?"

"You're right," she whispered, her tone low. She glared, and I backed away from the anger flashing in her eyes. "You are making a mistake. I wish this could've turned out differently."

"You're the one who's pushing me away over nothing."

"Nothing? You have no idea what you're doing.

None." She stormed past me, shoving my shoulder on the way. "See you around."

I stayed beneath the tree, confused by what just happened. Dagon appeared at my side, frowning down at me. "You okay?"

"Huh?"

"You have a weird look on your face."

"Uh, it's nothing. Just Kayla being difficult. She doesn't like you at all." I removed the enchanted necklace, smiling at Dagon's energy rushing in to surround me with a heat that was all him.

"Not surprised. You do realize your reaction to me being what I am isn't entirely normal."

"No, this is different," I told him. "You should've seen the look on her face when she was talking about you."

"I'm sorry. I know you were close."

"Don't apologize. There's no reason for her not to like you or to trust me for that matter." I slipped my hand into his and pulled him away from the tree. "Whatever. She wants to be stupid, that's on her. What's our plan for tonight?"

"Staying in, sadly."

"Not much of a change from how life was before all this shit," I assured him. "Though, it's better with you around. I don't get so bored, or talk to the walls, or do other things." I shook my head, thinking very clearly of how I'd spent some lonely nights in my apartment. He growled, and I laughed at the energy humming through our clasped hands.

"Morgan," he whispered.

"What?" I asked innocently. "Maybe you shouldn't be poking around my thought so much."

He let go of my hand to slip his arm around my waist instead. "You're going to regret that later."

"Hmm. I like the sound of that."

It was after one in the morning later that night that Dagon's snores drifted around my apartment. I tucked the blankets in around him better. I was glad he was getting some sleep, but I suddenly wasn't tired. He could use the rest. He hadn't been sleeping through the night since the attack at the farmhouse. I wasn't doing much better, but I also didn't have the added nightmares from visions of seeing the person I loved killed before my eyes. The notion that he'd witnessed my death had been scary. Every day since, though, my resolve to stop that vision from happening overrode my fear. I wasn't going to let my life be ruled by negative emotions, not any longer.

I adjusted my pillows, stilling when Dagon grunted in his sleep. A smile spread across his lips, and he murmured my name. I had no doubts about what he saw while he dreamed. He'd certainly found new ways to drive me crazy. We'd spent the evening snuggling on the couch afterward, watching whatever movies we hadn't gone through yet this week, and eating takeout from the local diner. He'd passed out soon as his head hit the pillow. I was wide awake and hoped reading my latest paperback would help me get to sleep. Another hour passed, and I decided I didn't need sleep tonight anyway. I was halfway through the book and was content to spend the rest of the night finishing it.

Dagon's growl vibrated through the bed. I put my bookmark in to hold my place and ran my fingers lightly through the hair around his horns. He settled, but the second I pulled away, he shot upright. I yelped, startled, and he cursed, slapping his hands to his face.

"Morgan," he whispered, the agony in his voice ripping through me.

"It's alright. I'm here. I'm right here." I scooted closer, holding him the best I could until the vision passed. It'd been a while since he'd had one. If he was saying my name, it probably wasn't about someone else being murdered.

That meant he was most likely watching me die. Again.

He curled in on himself, hugging his head to his knees. I squeezed him tighter, letting him know I was beside him. He shook, and his skin broke out in a cold sweat. He whispered my name, lifting his head. His eyes shimmered in the low light of the room, and he bundled me into his arms. His mouth crushed against mine in a frantic kiss while his hands tore at the blankets between us. He growled at the knit shorts I'd gone to bed in, his claws tearing through them and my panties beneath. I shoved at his briefs, pulling his shaft free and holding him firmly in my hands. He laid me down, spread my legs with his knee, and plunged inside.

His desperation to prove his vision hadn't come true yet seeped into me. I couldn't touch him enough. I dragged my nails down his back, his eyes becoming hooded with arousal. He grabbed hold of the metal headboard over my head and shifted to short, quick thrusts that had me bucking my hips, rising to meet him each time. I wrapped a leg around his waist, and he filled me all the way to the hilt over and over until I struggled to muffle my cry, and he groaned, his head falling to my shoulder. He slipped free and hugged me, both of us panting.

"Too real," he whispered. "They're becoming too real."

"Is it any different?" I traced the lines on his back, feeling it calm his nervous energy.

"No. There's a shadow, and it takes you from me. Why can't I stop it?"

"You will. We will. For tonight, just sleep."

He drifted off eventually, and I kept my arms around him through the night. A part of me was glad there hadn't been another murder yet. It did little to ease the worry that the vision of me dying was becoming more vivid each time he saw it. I couldn't shake the notion it meant the moment in question was going to happen soon. I spent the rest of the night listening to Dagon's breathing and trying not to panic that the life I could so clearly see with Dagon might be torn away, and there was nothing I could do to save it.

I CLIMBED out of the Tahoe, staring at the small, rundown cabin in the woods. "She lives here?"

Dagon laughed. "It's bigger on the inside."

I took his word for it, held his hand, and walked with him to the front door. We'd made it through another week of classes without another murder. Next week would be my last on campus. I didn't have any finals to sit for, thankfully, and just had to drop off papers and a few projects. I wasn't even sure Dagon had done any of his final work yet, but I didn't push him on it. He'd awakened every night this week from either a nightmare or another vision. He tried to put on a smile and pretend like he was fine.

He couldn't hide his emotions from me, not as easily as he used to. I hated how much he worried about me. Nothing I said or promised to do made it better. I took to simply being there for him when he woke up and doing my best not to leave his side during the day.

It was why today had me so off-kilter. Dagon had brought me to Cyrene's for two reasons. The first, so I could learn a bit more about what I could do. And the second was about leaving me in a safe location while he and his oldest brother went on the hunt for the monster. Cyrene had contacted us last night saying she'd tweaked a tracking spell to start searching for the beast. Search for it, but not go after it, not yet. For that, I was thankful. Watching Dagon almost torn to shreds haunted me every day. I'd spent so much time with him lately, the idea of him being out there even with his brother left me anxious.

At the front door, Dagon knocked. A crash sounded from inside, followed by laughing. "It's open!"

We entered the cabin, and my jaw dropped at what laid beyond it. The house I'd seen from the outside was an illusion. The inside was huge, the foyer reaching up at least two stories with a single chandelier hanging from its center. The walls were decorated in tapestries, paintings, feathery masks, and even a suit of armor that I was certain moved. Beneath my feet was a violet, cushy rug matching the paint barely visible on the walls behind all the other items. I grinned, tiny balls of light flittering around the foyer and disappearing deeper into the house.

"I could totally live here," I murmured.

"Of course you could. Everything's purple," Dagon said, kissing the back of my hand. "Cyrene?"

"Here," she called through her laughter. "Sorry about that, dears." She stepped out of a room with a shiny black door, but she wasn't alone.

At first, I thought it was a man, but the light hit his skin, and my eyes widened. His body was a gorgeous shade of forest green and covered in detailed tattoos of vines and leaves that curled up his arms and naked chest. He wore only a pair of black leather pants. He nodded, his eyes crinkling in a smile. They, too, were green, but shifting from pale to dark. Long silver hair was drawn back in several braids that trailed to the man's waist. He turned to Cyrene, kissed her on the cheek, and strolled down the hall, making a right at the end of it. A neon arrow hung on the wall with another below it stating: Saloon.

"Did we interrupt something?" Dagon asked, and I nudged him with my elbow. "What?"

Cyrene laughed, flipping her long braid over her shoulder and motioning us to follow her. "Rik and I were merely having a conversation."

"A conversation, huh?"

I rolled my eyes, but Cyrene bounced on her feet while she walked. "Who is he?"

"Rik? He's fae, dear."

"That's a fae?" I exclaimed.

"They come in all shapes and sizes. Rik has been with me for over two hundred years now." Cyrene sighed, taking a left at the end of the hall. "You can learn all about him in a bit. Where's your brother?" she asked Dagon, turning around once we entered a room that had me tilting my head back in awe.

"Should be here soon."

"You can look around," Cyrene told me with a grin.

I nodded, unable to stop staring at the sight surrounding me. Shelves that shouldn't have been able to stand were set in random places throughout the room. They were overloaded with so many books, most of them sagged in the middle. Vining plants with an array of colors from reds to blues covered the walls and ceiling, growing through the wooden slats. Ivy hung from the wooden beams overhead. Papers fluttered like birds, and more lights zoomed through the air. I spotted tiny sparkling wings and couldn't hold back my giddiness at being surrounded by so much magic. The energies in here called to my soul. I shut my eyes, soaking them in. It was the same experience as when I was with Dagon. I was comforted.

I was home.

"Morgan," Dagon whispered, a grin tugging at his lips and his eyes shimmering.

"What?"

"You're glowing."

I glanced down, blinking in surprise at the subtle violet and green glow emanating from my skin. I unzipped my jacket and shrugged out of it. "Is this magic?"

"What's inside you is reacting to what's here." Cyrene took my hand, and the glow brightened.

Finally, I was going to figure out how to work with this strange ability I was born with. I started to ask Cyrene questions. She answered them just as quickly, explaining to me how tapping into the energies around me would become easier with time. I also had to be careful. Tapping into them too much or too quickly could have terrible effects. Dagon's concerned growl broke through my excitement. I went to him, assuring him I wasn't planning on going all crazy magic mode.

Unless it meant saving him again. Then I might push the limits of what I could do.

A knock echoed around the house. A few seconds later, a demon entered the room led by Rik. Dagon went to him and shook his hand. "Morgan, this is Calrod. The oldest."

Where Dagon gave off a green aura and Arkon an amber one, Calrod was a deep shade of blue that reminded me of the sky just before night closed in. It matched his eyes. I shook the hand he offered, noting he was broader than Dagon and just as tall.

"Pleasure to meet you," Calrod said, his voice deep and gravelly.

"Heard a lot about you. Apparently, you control

fire?" Dagon had told me Arkon was adept at using magic while their other brother could wield one of the elements.

Calrod grinned and snapped his fingers. A flame sparked to life at his fingertips. "That I can."

"And he's also the best damned tracker I know," Dagon said. "You ready with that spell, Cyrene?"

"Remember," Cyrene told them, handing over a slip of paper with a smokey-colored crystal attached to it, "you're only tracking it. You're not to engage it, understand? We need to know what it is. Where it goes if anywhere when it's not murdering witches."

"And if we do find it?" Calrod asked.

"You gather what information you can about it, and you return. Whatever brought this darkness has openly declared war against witches. They're either extremely stupid, or far stronger and more clever than I assumed. Until I know which one, no one is to engage it. I'll not be patching you two up if you come back bloody," Cyrene warned. "Be smart about this. Right now, the creature is targeting Dagon. Let's not let it have what it wants."

"That'd be preferable," I agreed, crossing my arms.

Dagon handed the spell to Calrod, then came to me. He hugged me, breathing me in at the same time. "I'll be back before you know it. You're not to leave this house."

"You think I'd go anywhere else?" He kissed me and started to pull away until I tugged on his hand. His brow crinkled, and I pulled him into another hug, pressing my lips to his ear. "Watch out for your brother. His energy is riddled with sadness. He seems distracted. Don't let him get hurt."

Dagon promised he would and stepped back, eyeing Calrod. "Ready to go?"

Calrod held up the spell. "Let's go track us a beastie. Morgan."

"Be careful," I said, waving. They left the room, and I heard a door open then close down the hall. "Why's Calrod so sad? His energy felt so heavy."

"He fears he won't find the same happiness his brothers have." Cyrene sighed. "He's a fool."

"Why?"

"He's impatient. And he worries for his brothers, of course. Worries the lives they're building for themselves will be snatched away as they were before, and there's nothing he can do to stop it. He blames himself for what occurred in the Underworld. Thinks he's weak."

"Doesn't sound like it was his fault."

"Maybe not, but he's been carrying around that

guilt since the day they fled." She clapped her hands, then rubbed them together. "Enough chatting about Calrod. It's time to focus on you, my dear. Ready to get started?"

Three hours later and I sank to the floor in an exhausted heap. Cyrene clapped, ecstatic about the progress I'd made. I wasn't even sure I could call it an improvement. Rik was here, too. She'd had me work with both their emotions and their energies to learn how to control my ability. It was harder than I anticipated, but I was getting better at blocking what others felt instead of having it affect me. Once I mastered it, there'd be no more backaches, thankfully. Being an empath, Cyrene told me, was a gift as much as a curse. Eventually, I'd be able to use others' emotions to help show them their truest selves and embrace what they felt in their souls. Everyone was usually guilty of hiding from one emotion or another. Tucking them down for too long, she'd said, only caused more damage to the soul.

The energy reading was even harder to control. Apparently, she'd been holding herself in check since I arrived for my sake. Rik had done the same. Once they let me feel what their energies were really like, I'd been knocked off my feet.

I'd told Cyrene how I'd somehow tapped into

Dagon's energy a couple of times now. She'd said once I was stronger, I'd be able to do that with anyone I came into contact with. The stronger they were, the harder it'd be to do, and it'd only last a few seconds. Mastering such a skill would give me access to the same natural abilities of the person. At least now I knew how I'd managed to reach Jasmine so quickly after using Dagon's energy.

"You have years of practice ahead of you," Cyrene said, holding out her hand and hauling me to my feet. "That is if you wish to continue to learn."

"Why wouldn't I? I always believed I was messed up, but now that I know what this is, what I can do? Going back to my life before seems silly." I'd be able to stand in crowds again and embrace the energy around me instead of having it bombard me constantly. I could block it out if I wanted.

The more I looked around the room, taking in the vast array of items and books, the more it hit me. Going into anthropology, taking all those random classes on ancient religions, paganism had all led me here. Did I really want to go work at a dig site somewhere or in a museum? The human world and history were fascinating, but this was magic and demons and so much more than I ever dreamed possible. There was an entire world waiting for me to explore.

"You know," Cyrene said casually, "I've been needing someone to assist me with my magic. And this collection? It's a disaster." She waved her hand around the room. "I also hear the Witch Archives are always looking for fresh blood."

"There's a Witch Archives?" I asked, bouncing on my feet. "Where?"

"Far from here, but you can easily use magic to travel there and back. You wouldn't have to move out of state if you didn't want to. Just a suggestion."

"That'd be amazing."

I thought of Mack and Zane and my parents. I didn't want to tell them about magic and demons. I was sure they wouldn't understand—maybe one day way down the road. And if I could stay in Missouri, I wouldn't have to say goodbye to them. Now, if we could only figure out what was trying to kill me in Dagon's visions, I'd be able to throw myself entirely into the life I saw ready and waiting for me.

"How often are the visions coming?" Cyrene asked, her violet eyes darkening.

I frowned, and she winked. Having one mind-reader around was bad enough some days. Two almost made it pointless to speak. "Almost nightly now," I admitted. "He says they're getting worse. More vivid."

Cyrene moved through the room toward a table holding a crystal ball on a silver pedestal. She waved her hand over it, and the sphere filled with white smoke. She tilted her head, gripping the edge of the round table. The smoke morphed and twisted, but whatever it showed her, I hadn't the slightest idea. I picked up on her emotions instead. A sharp twist of fear jabbed into my back. I gasped the same time Cyrene did, and Rik was at her side in an instant. He stood behind her, reaching his arms around, so his hands covered hers. His worry drowned out Cyrene's emotions. The smoke turned black, and Cyrene staggered backward into Rik.

"The shadow draws closer," she whispered. "There's something wrong with it."

"Aside from it trying to kill me, you mean?"

Cyrene nodded, reaching for the sphere. "Voices. Too many voices clamoring to speak at the same time. They're in agony."

Rik caught her hand before she could touch it, and she shook her head as if clearing away a fog. He whispered in her ear, and she turned her back on the sphere.

I waited for her to say more, but the smoke faded altogether, and her shoulders sagged.

"Well, I could use a drink. Morgan?" Cyrene asked. "Besides, the brothers will be back soon."

I didn't bother to ask how she knew, too worried about what she'd seen in the crystal ball. We strolled through the house toward the room labeled *Saloon*. The swinging slatted doors were exactly as I pictured they'd be if we were in the old west. What awaited me inside was even better. It was like I'd stepped back in time. I wanted to ask why, out of all the themes she could've chosen, she went with a saloon, but Cyrene was speaking quietly with Rik. She sat down at the bar, and I joined her. Rik moved behind it, mixing a concoction that ended up dark green and glowing. Cyrene lifted the shot glass in a toast, and I did the same. The drink left my tongue tingling, and a burst of warmth shot all the way down to my toes, reenergizing me.

"That's better," Cyrene said, smacking her lips. "Ah, they're here."

The front door opened. Cyrene called to Dagon and Calrod, letting them know where we were. They entered the saloon, boots covered in mud and leaves. Neither appeared harmed, and I picked up on the aggravation right away.

"Nothing," Calrod grumbled, leaning on the bar. "Not a damned trace of anything out there."

"Did the spell not work?" I asked.

"Oh, it worked. Picked up on all sorts of magical traces left behind by a couple of sprites and a cluster of fairies, but none of them leading us to a monster or the murder sites, or evil." Calrod handed the spell to Cyrene, a defeated look in his eyes. I let down my guard to see his emotions and found the guilt Cyrene had mentioned earlier. I'd have to talk to Dagon about ensuring his older brother didn't let himself sink too low into despair.

"How'd everything go here?" Dagon asked, kissing my cheek.

"Good. I'm exhausted, but I'm learning. I have a few things I want to talk to you about later," I said, grinning.

"Am I going to like these things?"

"I think so." He wrapped his arms around me, resting his chin on my shoulder. "You look worn out, too."

"I just want this to be over."

I understood completely. Cyrene called for a round of drinks for everyone. "Since you're back, I suppose we should try to find out what this creature is the old-fashioned way," she said, lifting her shot glass full of the glowing, green liquid. "Who's ready for hitting the books?"

Hitting the books, in this case, meant opening some texts that tended to scare the shit out of me. Some screamed when you opened them. Others had words that flew right off the page and into your forehead. In most, the illustrations came to life and hopped onto the floor. Getting them back in their texts was a pain in the ass, though watching Dagon and Calrod chase around tiny drawings of goblins was amusing. We tore through Cyrene's collection of texts and scrolls. Still, nothing we came across resembled the monster that attacked us at the farmhouse.

Saturday night gave way to Sunday morning. Dagon had passed out with his head in my lap at one point while we sat on the floor surrounded by piles of leatherbound books. I'd smiled down at him while he slept, hoping the few hours he snagged would be peaceful. When he woke up, I took the chance to crash for an hour. Rik kept us supplied with food and drinks, giving Cyrene worried glances each time he entered the room. He never spoke, but he didn't have to for me to feel the depth of his love for his witch.

I was digging through another patch of loose

pages covered in dust and cobwebs, when my fingers brushed over something rough and scaly. My stomach twisted in knots, and I clapped a hand to my mouth, searching for a trashcan to be sick in. I made it in time, heaving while Dagon hurried over to hold my hair back.

"What happened?" he asked.

"I touched something," I said in between losing my lunch. "Felt like that monster, only worse."

Calrod frowned and went to where I'd been standing. He lifted the stack of papers aside, revealing a black scaled book. "This?" He held it up, and I grew light-headed. "Feels evil," he muttered. "Why do you have this lying around?"

Cyrene took it from him. "I have many texts in this house. Everyone reacts to them differently." She flipped through the pages, sighing until she reached the end of the book. Slowly, she spun it around, holding it open.

"That's it," Dagon snapped, his arms closing protectively around me as if the beast was going to leap off the page and attack.

When the illustration came to life, I clung to his arm. Our last encounter with the beast had left me shaken. I reached for the scars left behind by the monster's attack. They throbbed uncomfortably in recognition. "What is it?"

"An abomination," Cyrene whispered, her fury whipping through the room with a hot wind.

"Why does it look like a demon?" Calrod asked.

"Because at one point, it was one." Cyrene slammed the book down on the nearest table, her violet eyes glowing and her nails tapping loudly on the wooden surface. "This is old magic. Forgotten, or it used to be. This spell, in particular, has been forbidden, deemed too horrible to use."

"What's it do?"

Cyrene turned her gaze to me, and the wind gusted furiously around the room then stilled. Pages that been thrown into the air settled haphazardly on the shelves and floor. "A witch takes a demon, tortures him. Breaks him apart. She twists his soul until he's nothing but a mindless beast who knows only hunger for blood and rage. It takes more than one witch to create it, however. More than one witch to control it."

"Do you think there's a coven out there doing this?" Dagon asked. "Why would they use it to kill other witches?"

"I don't know. Witches and demons aren't born enemies. We had our differences centuries ago, but to go to this extent, this poor demon is being endlessly tortured." Cyrene shuddered, and Rik appeared at her side, smoothing his hands down her arms. She closed her eyes, whispering to him in a language I didn't understand. "If this is truly what we're dealing with, I can create a spell to track the beast. We need to put it out of its misery and stop whatever coven has decided to turn against its own."

The energy in the room weighed on my shoulders. The aura around Cyrene flared a bright purple before I sensed her closing herself off.

"I'll contact you once I have something," she informed us stiffly. "Until then, remain vigilant and get some rest while you can."

We took that as our cue to leave. I thanked Cyrene for starting my lessons. She managed a smile, but her strength had seemed to have gone out of her. The three of us walked to the front door and stepped out in time to catch the sun setting. Calrod made Dagon promise he'd contact him before he went after the monster again, hugged us both, and climbed onto his motorcycle. He took off down the old dirt road leaving Dagon and me alone. We got into the Tahoe and started the drive back to campus. Dagon held my hand the entire time, neither of us saying a word.

12

DAGON

Tonight should've been a night for celebrating. The semester was officially over for me and Morgan but going out didn't sit well with us. It'd been days since I had any visions. After having them so frequently, not seeing anything had an uneasy weight settling in my gut.

Morgan shifted in my arms, and I held her closer, running my claws lightly down her spine. We laid in bed at her place, soaking in each other's warmth. We'd spent the evening trying to chase away our impatience of not having a way to go after the beast yet, or the coven behind it. Cyrene had said she was close, but it'd be another few days. A few more days of waiting to see if another witch was murdered.

Another day of waiting to see if it'd come after

Morgan or me.

"I should probably give Cyrene an answer soon."

I frowned, glancing down at Morgan's eyes staring up at me. "About?"

"Working at the Witch Archives."

"I don't see why you shouldn't do it." I hugged her, kissing the top of her head. We'd been lying here for the last couple of hours, talking quietly and holding onto each other. I could certainly get used to evenings like this. "What would you tell your family about your new job?"

She shrugged, planting a kiss on my collar bone and inching her way slowly higher. "I'll come up with someone. Don't think they're ready for the whole, hey I'm in love with a demon, and oh yeah, I'm a witch, too. That might be a bit much."

My hands stilled on her back. I grinned, replaying those words in my mind. I dipped into her thoughts, sinking right into a memory of her watching over me while I slept. What she felt in that moment radiated from her now. I lowered my mouth to hers, kissing her deeply and taking my time drawing out quiet moans of pleasure. I ripped through the thin cotton panties she'd worn to bed and tossed them aside.

"You're going to have to take me shopping," she

murmured, lifting her hips to mine after I'd laid her out beneath me. "That's the fifth pair of underwear you've shredded."

"Maybe you should just stop wearing clothes to bed. Or in your apartment."

"We'd never leave."

I looked down at her, spreading her legs with my knee. "And?"

She started to speak until I gently rocked forward. She cupped her breasts, tugging her nipples while my hand sought out her bead. Leisurely I massaged the tender flesh, falling even harder for Morgan with every little noise she made and every tiny shift of her body reacting to mine. Our release came abruptly and together, crashing into each other while I buried myself within her sheath. She let out a breathy laugh, cupping my face and kissing me.

When she fell asleep a little while later, I let my fingers trail down her arm to her hip, memorizing every curve and freckle. I was close to falling asleep until a tapping sound came from the window. Carefully, I untangled my legs from Morgan's and slid to the edge of the bed. I tugged on my gym shorts and hurried to the window. A paper crane sat on the stone ledge outside. I opened the window, and it fluttered inside, landing on my hand. The paper unfurled, and I read the message left in curling handwriting.

My heart sank, and I slumped onto the loveseat, glancing at Morgan peacefully sleeping.

The message was from Cyrene. She'd cooked up a spell to track the magic needed to create the monster. It'd be ready in the morning. I should've been thrilled, but the concern I'd been fighting for days left my palms sweaty and my claws and fangs threatening to lengthen. We were one step closer to finding the monster, which meant we were potentially one step closer to witnessing my vision of Morgan coming true.

I snagged my cell off the coffee table and texted Calrod. He replied not long after, saying he'd meet me at Cyrene's first thing in the morning. I crumpled up the note and tossed it onto the table beside my phone.

Slowly, I padded through the silver light flooding in through the window and reached the bed. Morgan's brow crinkled, and she whispered my name. I tugged the blankets up around her and kissed her forehead. If she were with Cyrene, she'd be safe. I'd take her with us, give her some more time to work with her magic and hopefully, stay far away from the monster trying to kill us. After pacing around the apartment for a half-hour, attempting to get my rising anger and fear under control, I gave up and climbed back into bed. Morgan rolled over, hugging me to her even while she slept. I thought of the vision I had showing our future, praying thinking of that moment would calm me down.

Instead, it left me wide-awake, holding Morgan as tight as I could. No matter what happened today, this couldn't be our last night together.

"ARE you sure you're up for this today?"

I glanced at Calrod, then over my shoulder at the front door to Cyrene's home. Morgan was safely tucked away inside. I had the new spell and potion in my hands, ready to be used. The magic hummed through me, far more potent than the last tracking spell she'd given us.

"Dagon?"

"Yeah, I'm good," I growled.

He pursed his lips, only looking away from me when tires crunched over gravel. Jasmine's jeep appeared, and Arkon climbed out from behind the wheel. We'd tried to talk him out of coming, but he wouldn't listen. At least he'd managed to convince Jasmine to stay behind. Arkon took one look at me and crossed his arms.

"Don't even say it," I snapped. "I can handle this. We going, or what?"

Not waiting for an answer, I stomped to my SUV, got in, and waited. Calrod and Arkon joined me, and I set off, not looking back at the witch's home. Morgan was safe with Cyrene. They were going to spend the day doing more training and coming up with a way to save the demon forced to murder witches.

Nothing was going to get into that house or through the layers of warding around it.

The drive back to campus took a little over an hour, with none of us speaking. I parked in one of the less used lots and stepped out, Arkon and Calrod right behind me. I figured a good place to start was the dead clearing and set off into the woods. With the semester over for most students, the college grounds were emptier than usual. The students remaining were either busy cleaning out their apartments and dorms or finishing up whatever finals they had left. I paused at the tree line. I'd been so busy thinking about taking down the beast, I hadn't bothered to consider what Morgan and I would do over the summer. The idea of her going back home with Mack and not being near me had me growling. Would she be okay with moving in together if I asked? We'd essentially been living that way the last few weeks, but that was a huge step.

"Dagon?" Calrod nudged my arm.

"Sorry, just uh, thinking. I forgot to handle a few issues," I mumbled.

We'd take care of the beast, and whatever coven of witches thought they could wreak havoc like this and get away with it. Then I'd panic over moving in together.

Once inside the trees, we jogged to the clearing. I wanted to get back to Morgan and had no doubt Arkon was in the same boat. We stepped up to the dead tree, and I breathed in deep. There were no scents left behind of recent magic or any new candles or designs left on the ground.

"Right, let's do this." I handed over the potion and spell to Arkon, figuring he might be able to give it a bigger kick since he used magic.

He popped the cork out of the small, glass vial holding the shimmering gold powder and recited the spell. The words were written in a language I didn't understand, but the powder glowed and floated out of the vial. It twisted in the air like a mini cyclone, then circled the clearing three times. It coiled back in on itself, flared brighter, and zoomed into the trees, leaving a faint shimmering trail behind it.

With Calrod in the lead, we followed the magical trace darting around trees and through bushes. It paused at the locations the bodies had been found, then set off again. When it turned sharply, heading toward campus, I cursed. Were the witches students?

How close had they come to Morgan without me knowing it?

Ensuring our glamours were still in place, we traipsed out of the woods and headed across campus. The shimmering trail went unnoticed by the humans, oblivious to the magic occurring around them. We wove around them, me growling when they didn't get out of the way fast enough. The trail ran right into the doors of Morgan's building, and my lip twitched.

"Keep it together," Arkon warned in an undertone. "Your face is starting to show."

"Morgan lives here," I uttered, forcing the glamour back into place.

Calrod's eyes sparked with fire. He reached for the door, yanked it open, and led the way inside. The trail led to the stairs, and we took them two at a time.

It guided us to one floor above Morgan's apartment and down the hall. The shimmering powder stopped outside a door, darting up and down, but couldn't seem to go any further. I rushed forward but was stopped by Arkon yanking my arm back.

"What?"

"Magic," he whispered, glaring at the door. "Heavy magic. The door's got a trap on it."

"We have to figure out who lives here."

"Let me deal with it. Just hang on."

I glanced up and down the hall, but we were alone. Calrod kept watch to the left and me to the right while Arkon cautiously approached the apartment door. He was within a foot when a bright blue spark exploded, aiming for him. He darted back, snarling at the magic attempting to keep him away. The entire door came to life, a shifting mess of blue electricity. Arkon's eyes narrowed, then he snapped his fingers, whispering in demonic. An amber orb of light flew from his hand to the door, crashing into it. He did it a second and third time, wearing down the magical trap until finally, the spell broke, and the door was left smoking. Tentatively, he reached out and grabbed the knob.

With one hard twist and shoving his shoulder into the door, it opened with a loud crack. We hustled inside and closed ourselves in. The apartment was a one-bedroom, and we spread out. Arkon took the bedroom, Calrod the living room, and I took the kitchen area. The space reeked of magic, though there was nothing out in the open to designate a witch lived here. I was about to sort through the stack of papers on the table in the kitchen when Arkon called from the bedroom. He stood in front of an open closet, his eyes glowing and his claws tearing through the paint of the doors he clutched in his hands. I peered over his shoulder and snarled.

An image of the twisted demon stared back at me from an effigy created out of clay and stone. Surrounding it were various symbols that had been painted in black and red paint on the wall. A small, black table sat beneath it with a cast-iron bowl in the middle. Various smokey crystals surrounded it, with black candles in between. Burnt herbs were all that remained in the bowl, too far gone for me to figure out what they were.

"I thought Cyrene said a coven was needed to bring that thing to life," Calrod murmured.

"I think it did," Arkon replied, nodding to the right side of the closet. "Are those what I think they are? Gods, who is this person?"

Attached to the wall in three rows were

photographs of people—men and women. I leaned in, a flash of familiarity hitting me when I saw the last seven that were there. I'd seen their faces in visions right before they were killed. I had no idea how I hadn't seen the first five. Hanging from the wall were small plastic bags, each one covered in dried blood. Inside were slivers of what appeared to be chunks of meat and hair. I didn't want to get any closer, but I had to know what was inside of them. I removed one of the twelve bags and opened it. The stench turned my stomach, and I shut it as fast as I could.

"Heart," I said, then gagged. "It's part of a heart and someone's hair."

"Twelve bags," Calrod mused. "The members of a coven? Aren't there usually thirteen?"

"Depends on the coven." I dropped the bag on the floor, gagging again at the wet sound it made when it hit. "We need to show this to Cyrene."

Arkon took out his cell and snapped pictures of the effigy and the bags. Hoping somehow it'd be easy to destroy the monster stalking Wellsville and threatening Morgan, I grabbed the statue and threw it to the ground. It shattered, but there was no burst of magic. No indication I'd done anything to stop the threat.

"If you hadn't done it, I would have," Arkon said, grinding the heel of his boot into the pieces that remained.

I turned away from the closet and tore through the bedroom. I was about to give up and head back to the living room until I spotted a photograph sticking out of a journal I'd tossed to the floor. Crouching, I picked it up, and the pages fell open.

"Shit," I spat, tossed the journal on the bed, and fumbled for my phone. I hit Morgan's name and clutched the phone in my hand while it rang. "Pick up, damn it. Come on, answer. Please answer."

Arkon and Calrod gave me confused glances, then they looked at the picture on the bed. Morgan's smiling face stared back at me from the glossy image. And right beside her, grinning like she was the most innocent person in the world, was Kayla.

There was no answer. I hung up and called again. Cyrene's place was impossible to find, let alone break into. Then again, if Kayla was somehow using the combined strength of her coven, I had no idea how formidable she'd be. Had she slaughtered her own coven for power? The phone rang, and just when it was about to go to voicemail again, Morgan's voice came on the line.

"Hey, sorry, didn't hear—"

"Where are you?" I demanded, cutting off Morgan's words.

"At Cyrene's. Why? What's wrong?"

"Is she with you? I need to talk to her."

"Yeah, she's standing right here. Hang on." There was a bit of static, then Morgan said, "She's here. You're on speaker."

"Is your place safe?" I asked.

"Of course it's safe," Cyrene snapped. "Did you find something?"

"You could say that. Do not let Morgan leave."

"Dagon? You're freaking me out here," Morgan said. "What did you find?"

Static filled the line again. Morgan's voice cut in and out. The static grew louder, then horrible high-pitched laughter came through.

"No," I whispered, listening to the sound grow louder. "No!"

"Dagon?" Arkon asked.

"It's there," I whispered. "Morgan? Answer me! Morgan?"

Through the static and cackling, Morgan screamed. There was another shout that sounded like Cyrene, then the line went dead.

I stared horrified at my phone, the silence crushing the air from my lungs.

My mouth was dry, and my head throbbed. I tried to reach up to rub my eyes, but my arms were held in place by something. Rope? I pried open one eye, squinting around. I sat on a metal chair, my legs bound just like my arms. Where was I? I'd been at Cyrene's, hadn't I? I tugged against the ropes, but there was no give.

"Think," I whispered, glancing around. What else happened?

My phone. My phone had rung, hadn't it? And Dagon, he'd been calling me, but everything after that was fuzzy. The room seemed familiar. More metal chairs like the one I sat in were the only furniture I could make out in the dim lighting. The floor beneath my feet was linoleum with a diamond-shaped blue pattern. Shit, I was on campus. This had to be a classroom, or maybe a storage room? My heart plummeted and panic set in. The murderer. How had he gotten past Cyrene's warding? There was an explosion at her front door, then that beast had charged in. A swell of shadows had swarmed the house and then, nothing.

Dagon was probably losing his mind right now. Shit. I had to get out of here.

Sunlight outlined the wall of windows, the blinds pulled tightly shut. A rustling came from behind, and I jumped. More of the confused haze that had filled my mind when I came to dissipated, and I picked up on the energies in the room. One was faint, but I recognized it as Cyrene's. Did I dare call her name? Something else was here, too, something heavier. I hated to do it, but the room was too dark to make much out anyway. I shut my eyes, concentrating on what the energy tried to tell me. It was strange not to pick up anything from the students who remained on campus. Wherever we were, we had to be far enough away for me not to feel them. Or whoever had taken me put up some kind of magical block.

I gave my head a little shake, wincing at the pain

it caused, and focused again. The air was thick and smelled musty. I thought something might be burning, but the scent faded as quickly as it came. The energy pulsed, reaching out to touch me.

My stomach roiled, and I threw my head to the side, vomiting from the contact. The same press of sickening delight that could only come from something evil landed on my shoulders and smashed into my temples. I dry-heaved, groaning at the pain in my torso and from the ropes burning into the bare skin at my wrists. A cold sweat broke out on my forehead, and I shook violently on the chair so badly it scooted across the floor and threatened to topple over until I managed to right myself. Remembering Cyrene's lessons, I tried to cut off my connection to the negative energy, but nothing worked. It clung to my skin like a sticky syrup oozing over my flesh and seeping into my pores.

The energy stung ice-cold. Steps came closer, and I froze, willing myself not to scream at what crept up behind me. Without turning, I knew what it was. I wouldn't yell. I wouldn't do it.

A clawed hand stretched into view at my right, and I bit back a shout. The wicked sharp talons curled toward me, a monstrous, deep-throated growl at my ear. Hot breath burned the back of my neck, and a quiet whimper slipped past my lips. The beast snatched the chair and whipped me around. It snarled in my face, and thinking of Dagon, I shouted right back at it, not about to let fear take root. Saliva dripped from its fangs that were far too large for its mouth. Rancid breath hit my face, and I gagged. It gripped the seat of the chair and my thighs, its weight threatening to break the bones.

Red eyes pierced mine. They glowed, lighting up the area around us. Something shiny glinted to my left, but I didn't dare look away. Its mouth yawned open, and I pulled harder at the ropes, not about to be eaten by this thing. Somewhere amid its growling and my yelling, I picked up on an emotion that wasn't mine. It was hard to zero in on, but sadness flickered through me, so much sadness and pain.

Was it coming from the beast?

"Stop," a voice called, and the monster stilled. It snapped its jaws shut and leaned back but didn't release the chair. "You've scared her enough."

The voice was a mix between a man and a woman, but it sounded familiar.

"Who are you?" I tentatively shifted my gaze from the creature. All I could see were shadows around me. "Really? We're going to play that game?

Why don't you just come out, huh? Why bother hiding? We both know you're going to kill me."

Laughter struck me like stinging bees. "If I wanted you dead, you'd be dead."

"Then what do you want?"

The shadows moved, and I gulped. Shit. This person, this thing, it had to be what Dagon had seen in his visions. The same shadow that consumed me. No matter what he, or she or whoever it was might say, there was a high probability I was about to die.

That was just perfect.

"I want you to join me."

"Sorry, what?"

"You heard me, Morgan Nelson. I've been watching you for some time now. It's quite clear to me how strong you are. How powerful. I seek to rebuild my coven and you, I'd hoped you would be the perfect new addition."

"Coven? I thought you already had once since you conjured this abomination," I spat.

The beast growled, but the same wave of sadness I'd sensed earlier hit me again, stronger this time. Cyrene had explained how a demon had to be taken and twisted to make this monster. That he was constantly tortured by the magic corrupting his soul. He was still in there somewhere. If I could tap into his energy, was there a way to free him? Free us both?

A grunt came from across the room, and the shadow sighed. "Be quiet. I'll deal with you soon enough."

I wasn't sure who it was talking to when the monster shifted to his right. "Cyrene!"

She glared at the mass of shadows from behind the silver bars of a cage suspended from the ceiling. Her arms and legs were trapped in iron sleeves, and a gag covered her mouth. It, too, was metal, and from the redness of her face, it appeared to be burning her. Her eyes widened, but there was no violet glow I'd become used to seeing. I sensed none of her energy at all.

"What did you do to her?" I demanded, and the shadows moved again, shifting more into the form of a person wearing a cloak.

"I trapped her."

The voice was more feminine now, teasing me. I knew who was under that cloak. I turned all my attention to the figure, fighting against the instinct telling me not to look away from the beast who could easily chomp me in half. There was hardly any energy coming from the shadow, almost as if Kayla was here with me. The second I thought her name, I leaned back, my jaw dropping in disbelief.

"It can't be," I whispered. "Kayla?"

The figure threw the hood back, revealing the face of someone I thought I'd known. Kayla's eyes glowed crimson, and her wicked smile made my pulse race. "I'm impressed. Such power is hidden inside you, Morgan. How could you not have known you were a witch all this time?"

"I just didn't. Wait, I don't understand. Why are you doing this? How did you even find us?"

Kayla's lips screwed up in a vicious sneer. "I have my ways. She might be older than me, but even she isn't stronger than an entire coven."

I glanced around, but no other witches appeared from the shadows. "Where is your coven?"

Kayla dragged the cloak apart, then lifted the pendant hanging from around her neck. It shimmered with blues and greens. A high-pitched keening sound filled my ears, and a swarm of hatred, fear, and agony ripped right through me. It was as if more people had flooded into the room, their energies competing to be known, though no physical bodies appeared. "They're with me, and they always will be."

Cyrene shouted, but the noise was muffled.

Kayla rolled her eyes, continuing to fiddle with the charm while she turned to face Cyrene.

"I'm sorry, did you want to say something?" Kayla shrugged. "Too bad. No more casting for you. Might as well stop trying to yell at me."

Cyrene's eyes narrowed, and her body jerked against the restraints. None of them gave.

"What did you do?" I whispered. "Those are their souls, aren't they? I can feel them."

"You're a fast learner. My coven brought ruin to themselves just as I knew they would, just as you're doing without even realizing it." Kayla sighed, striding toward me. She waved her hand, and the beast moved to stand behind my chair. "Now, I'm going to give you one chance to stop this foolish fling you have with Dagon and join me."

"You're joking, right?"

The slap came out of nowhere, and my head flew to the left. The strong taste of blood filled my mouth, and a second backhand jostled my already throbbing head. "Don't be an idiot," Kayla seethed. She grabbed a handful of my hair and yanked my head back. My hands tightened around the arms of the chair, but the ropes remained taut. "They thought demons could be trusted, too. Our elder fell in love with one of their kind. He was using her for her magic. I warned her demons couldn't love. They're nothing but mindless beasts." Her eyes darkened, and she whispered, "They killed my parents when I was a child. Right in front of me. Then our elder goes and gives her heart to one."

She scoffed, her hand wrapping around my throat.

"She was so like you. So ready to throw herself away. I had to stop her from destroying herself, from destroying us all." She released my throat with a sigh, a mad gleam appearing in her eyes.

"Kayla, what did you do?" I whispered.

"There was an accident," she mused. "Magic can be dangerous. Our poor elder was killed, as were the strongest of our coven." She shifted her gaze to the demon she'd turned into her personal weapon and grinned. "Their power was more than enough for me to teach this demon a lesson. The demon who thought he could hold the heart of a witch."

He was the one who'd fallen in love with the elder? The sadness coming from him, the pain, now I knew where it stemmed from. "Why?"

"My coven lost their way."

"So you cursed an innocent demon to murder the rest of your coven?" I yelled, putting the rest of the pieces together. The witches that were killed, they had to be what remained of her family. "You're sick."

"Innocent?" she bellowed. "None of them were innocent. They let others influence their magic and get inside their heads. Demons aren't the only ones who try to constantly take advantage of us. My coven didn't understand what they were doing to themselves. To their magic."

"And that gives you the right to slaughter them?"

"I'm the only one who sees what's happening," she whispered, tugging on the pendant. "The only one who sees that our world is changing. The demons and fae, all they want is our magic. Even a witch such as her has fallen for their lies, living with a fae. Claiming he loves her. They want to steal what we have. You, I can save you, Morgan. It's why I hid my energy from you, to give you someone you could be around. Someone you could feel safe with." She nodded wildly, her hair dancing around her head. "Please, let me save you. I just want a new family to call my own. You've let yourself be manipulated, just as my elder did. Once I kill him, you'll see. Dagon is the true villain. All demons are."

I gaped at her. She'd lost her mind. How had I not realized how insane she was all this time? "You murdered your coven," I whispered. "Kayla, I'm not the one who needs help. You do."

She stilled, and the temperature in the room plummeted. The shadows massed behind her, seeping from the cloak. "You could've been a great witch. The power we could've had together would've been unstoppable. It's high-time the witches return to their true seat of power."

"I won't let you kill Dagon," I said, tugging on the ropes.

She raised her hands, her palms glowing a sickly green. "I'm afraid you won't be around to stop me. Goodbye, Morgan."

I tried tapping into Kayla's energy, but there was nothing there for me to hold onto. The glow in her hands brightened. Cursing, I curled in on myself, waiting for the inevitable blow that would end my life.

A door banged open, and a furious roar filled the room.

Kayla screamed.

Her body sailed across the room and crash into the wall. A fireball shot through the air, nailing her in the chest, and she hit the wall a second time, screaming furiously. The creature threw back its head, roaring, then charged the door. A glowing green figure met it halfway and, with one hit, sent the beast staggering away.

"Rik?"

The fae that had seemed so docile the last time I'd seen him looked nothing like the kind, peaceful being I'd met. His eyes glowed, and when he opened his mouth, a hiss escaped. Two sets of fangs had grown in his mouth, and the tattoos on his body whirled and shifted, coming alive. Three figures ran into the room after him. I sighed in relief when Dagon and Arkon reached me, quickly cutting through the ropes with their claws.

Dagon yanked me out of the chair and into his arms, squeezing me tight.

"How'd you find us?"

He set me on my feet, cupping my face while he examined it. "We were headed back to the house when we ran into Rik. He'd been left behind. Guess they thought he was dead. He picked up Cyrene's trail. We followed him here."

Kayla was shouting at the creature to attack. Dagon shoved me behind him, and Arkon stood at his side. Rik and Calrod were working at breaking Cyrene out of the cage, but they weren't there yet. We had to give them time. And the demon, we had to free him and the souls of Kayla's coven. The moment I thought it, Dagon gave me a look over his shoulder.

"You can't be serious," he snapped.

"He's innocent, so are they," I argued. "We can't just leave them to suffer."

His clenched jaw and the pleading in his eyes told me he really wished I wasn't such a good person. "Do you have an idea of how to do either without all of us dying?"

"Maybe?"

"Morgan."

"What? Cyrene and I were talking about it before the house was attacked. I just need—"

"No!"

Dagon's fingers slipped through mine, and then I was torn away from him. Tendrils wrapped around my legs and then my wrists, dragging me across the floor and through the stacks of chairs.

A mass of shadows had taken over Kayla. She was a twisting blob of twisted magic, ready to devour me.

Dagon shouted, and I fought to get free, but the shadows only tightened more. The darkness rose up, hit the ceiling, then crashed down, plunging me into a black abyss.

Morgan disappeared into the raging storm of shadows. I shouted for her, but there was no answer. My vision was coming true right before my eyes. I was going to lose Morgan.

I started to lunge forward, but Arkon snatched my shoulder. He shoved me to the side, barely avoiding the slash from the monster attacking. It wasn't going to keep me from Morgan. I didn't care what she said about him being innocent. He was in the way.

A fireball struck the creature in the chest. It snorted, stomping its hooved foot on the floor. The fur burned away from where Calrod's attack struck, but it didn't stop him. The beast threw back his head and charged after us. We scattered, and Arkon nailed it with a slash of his claws down its back. Metal clanged. I turned, noting Rik had Cyrene free of the cage and cradled in his arms. Her legs, arms, and face were bright red and appeared to be blistered from whatever contraption Kayla had held her in. I yelled for Rik to get her out of here.

If Cyrene couldn't fight, she was only going to get in the way.

I dodged an attack thanks to Arkon's warning and worked my way around the edge of the room. Morgan hadn't reappeared yet from the mass of shadows, but she was alive. I found her mind and dove into the mad tangle of thoughts waiting for me. Desperation and fear nearly drove me to my knees, but it was the idea that came next that had me yelling for Rik to stop. He did, just outside the door, clutching Cyrene to his chest. Her eyes fluttered open, and she whispered something to him. He didn't take another step, and Cyrene didn't seem confused at all about why I needed her to stay.

"Come on," I whispered, remaining connected to Morgan. "Don't leave me. Don't let her win."

Through the shadows, I glimpsed a dark green light, striving to break free. The creature blocked my view, striking me in the gut with its arm. I was thrown head over heels and slammed into the far wall. Arkon and Calrod continued to fight the monster, doing their best to keep it away from me. More light broke through the shadows, and Morgan's mind became consumed with it. A scream that wasn't hers ripped through the room. The green light jutted outward like vines searching for the sun. They formed cracks in the darkness, breaking it into pieces until finally, I spotted Morgan's form. She was on her hands and knees, her head raised, and her eyes, gods, her eyes were of a predator.

What was left of the shadows condensed until there was only Kayla left standing wearing a black cloak. "You bitch," she snarled at Morgan, new shades fighting to grab purchase in the floor.

The energy Morgan took from Cyrene was too intense and snapped them like twigs. She pushed to her knees then finally stood. Shimmering green and white lights flowed around her body. I blinked, unsure if I was seeing things or had Morgan suddenly grown horns. Was she tapping into both of us? She was going to burn out if she didn't stop.

"Please, Kayla, just let them go," Morgan said.

Kayla's cackle stung my skin. I was on my feet, ready to tackle her and be done with it until she reached up and clasped the pendant hanging from her neck. An explosion of power erupted from her. An icy wind whipped around the room, sending us all flying back toward the door. Morgan yelped, crashing into a window. Glass shattered, and she toppled over, falling onto the shards.

"So much to learn." Kayla hovered off the floor several feet, the shadows quickly returning to mass behind her. They split into their own beings and stepped forward, standing beside the creature she'd made out of her fear and anger. "If only you'd chosen me instead of him, I could teach you." She raised her hand then let it fall. The line of shadows charged us down.

I scrambled across the floor, reaching Morgan. I curled my body around hers, ready to take the hits for her, only they never came. A wall of vines and flowers erupted from the floor, stretching to the ceiling. Cyrene knelt with her palms on the linoleum and Rik right beside her. She lifted her gaze to Morgan and nodded.

Morgan squeezed my hand. Blood oozed from various wounds covering her face and arms, and she was weakening from using so much magic. "I need you," she whispered, cringing each time she moved.

"We need to run," I growled, but she grabbed my shoulders and stared into my eyes.

"Help me get inside his head. I know how to stop this." Her eyes could barely stay open, and her hold on me faltered. I held her upright, wanting to throw her over my shoulder and flee.

Arkon and Calrod sidled closer, readying their next attacks. The shadows and the abomination beat at the wall of vines. They weren't going to hold forever. Going against instinct raging at me to get Morgan away from that evil witch, I gave in with a snarl.

"What do you need me to do?"

"Get inside his head when I tell you."

She didn't give me any further explanation. She shut her eyes, sucked in a deep breath, and held out her hand toward the wall of vines. More broke off and died on the floor. A shadow's hand slipped through, followed by its shoulder. They were going to be on us soon enough. Morgan's face scrunched, and she cursed. When she trembled and doubled over, I kept her steady, willing her to use my energy. As if reading my mind for once, she squared her shoulders, her back going ramrod straight. Her eyes flew open, and it was like I looked in a mirror.

"I have him," she said, her words raspy. A wispy tendril of red smoke drifted from the wall of vines to her hand then wound up her arm. "Take my hand

and show him his truth. Remind him who he is. He needs to break free of her hold."

I didn't stop to question if this would work. We were out of time. Two more of the shadows were preparing to break through. Calrod shot fire at them while Arkon kept them at bay with tiny explosions. They shrieked and withdrew, only to be replaced by more. I took Morgan's hand. The smoke quickly shifted to cover my arm. I followed it back to the demon who'd been twisted and turned into a vicious killer against his will.

The last time I'd been near him, I hadn't been able to see inside his head. With Morgan guiding me, I shoved past the shadows that were Kayla's magic and fell into a pit of grief and sadness that threatened to swallow me whole. Memories flitted past me of the demon's life before Kayla captured him. He'd been kind and loving. There'd been someone he loved in his life, a witch. I saw the two of them together and felt his pain the day he discovered her body, learned she'd been murdered. Worse was when I witnessed the night he killed his first victim.

His howl of rage and agony turned into my own. Anger burned through my veins at the face staring back at me. Kayla had made him kill innocents, witches he'd known and been close to. He'd given himself over to the darkness and despair then.

Now it was time for him to come back.

Holding Morgan's hand in mine, I directed his innermost emotions and energy back into him, forcing him to feel it. Forcing him to embrace who he once was. The shadows fought back, but with Morgan keeping a firm hold of me, I pushed back harder, using our combined energy to stay connected to the demon within. More memories appeared around me, filled with laughter and love until finally, I came face to face with the demon. His eyes widened, staring right at me. He clutched a hand to his chest, then opened his mouth wide and roared.

The connection shattered, and I collapsed to the floor with Morgan.

"What are you doing?" Kayla shouted.

Through the holes that had been made in the vines, I watched the demon tear through the shadow beings with his claws. They screamed while they died, turning into nothing but wisps. When the last one vanished, the wall of vines shattered. Cyrene's strength must've given out.

"Get back." Kayla raised her hand, but the demon didn't stop. He lifted his claws, going right for her. She ordered him away, but he slashed down her front. Blood spurted, and Morgan cursed. I hugged her to me, tucking her face against my chest, so she didn't have to watch. The demon tore into Kayla until there was nothing left of the witch but a bleeding, twitching body on the floor. She panted for air, her eyes wide, while the light quickly faded from their depths. Blood bubbled on her lips, and she let out one final sigh.

The demon stumbled toward us, shaking his head. Parts of his body crumpled like stone. He nodded to me and collapsed in on himself, becoming nothing more than a pile of dust. A blue, shimmering light remained behind, taking the shape of who the demon had been before he was cursed. He waved, then faded from view.

"The necklace," Morgan whispered, lifting her head. I tried to hold her back, but she forced herself forward. "I can do it."

Staying by her side, I walked across the room with her to Kayla's unmoving body. Blood drenched her clothes. The black cloak had turned to tatters without her magic to hold the shadows in place. Morgan crouched and lifted the pendant from a shallow pool of blood. With a quick yank, she broke the chain and straightened.

"How do we release them?"

Cyrene appeared at her side, Rik's arm firm around her waist. "I'll see their souls get to where they belong." She held out her hand, and Morgan dropped the necklace into it. "I certainly hope you return to your studies soon. There is great potential within you, both of you," she added, glancing to me. "Now, might I suggest we clean up this mess and leave before the humans come running?"

It was over. The vision of Morgan dying had come and gone, yet here she was alive and in my arms where she belonged. I hugged her, kissing the top of her head while she squeezed me back hard enough to hurt. I'd take whatever pain as long as it meant she was with me.

"THERE. LOOKS LIKE IT DID, MOSTLY." Morgan wiped her hands on her jeans, cleaning off the dust.

We stood in Cyrene's library, where we'd been for the last couple of days. Kayla's shadows had done a number on the place during the attack. While Cyrene recovered, Morgan and I offered to help straighten her home and get it back in some semblance of order. The souls of Kayla's coven had been released without any trouble. The heart slivers and hair had been discovered by the local authorities in Kayla's rooms, along with her body. We'd left it all in the woods by the old oak tree. The papers were having a field day with it.

Not that I cared. The whole mess was over. I slipped my hand into Morgan's, spun her around, and right into my body. She grinned, kissing me. I peered into her thoughts, and my hands slipped to her ass.

"Good thing Cyrene gave us a guest room," she murmured, gasping when I felt her up. "Dagon."

"You started it."

"Yeah. You going to finish it?" she teased.

"Soon enough. Did you decide?"

She beamed. "I did. Talking to the witches in charge next week, and I need to stay nearby to keep studying with Cyrene. I'm sure Arkon and Jasmine would love to have us nearby, too. And Calrod said he was looking for some extra handyman help..." She trailed off, her cheeks turning bright red.

"What is it?" This time when I tried to look into her thoughts, I was blocked. Cyrene must've been teaching her a few tricks the last couple of days.

Morgan reached into her back pocket and pulled out a piece of paper. "In case you missed the hint, I think I want us to stay in Oak Hollow. And, well, seems stupid to live separately."

I unfolded the paper, staring at the listing for a small cottage to rent just outside town. "You want to move in together?"

"Only if you want. Let's be real here. My life isn't exactly going to be focused on anthropology anymore or working in a museum. And I know you'd be happier if you were close to your family. Mine's not that far away and—"

I captured her mouth in a kiss, backing her into the nearest wall. "Yes, absolutely yes."

"Good, because I sort of already put down a deposit on the place. We can move in next week."

I smoothed the back of my hand over her cheek. There were no visible remnants of the fight thanks to Cyrene, but I saw the blood there all the same. She was a fighter, we both were, and nothing was going to take us away from each other. With a mad giggle, she slipped out of my arms, dodging around shelves and out the door. I caught up to her as she stood on the front porch.

"The moon's full, and there's a lot of woods around here," she mused, her brow arching.

I growled, seeing exactly what she had in mind. With another laugh, she took off into the woods. I gave her a few seconds head start then raced out after her.

Tomorrow we could work out our plan for moving.

Tonight, I was going to love Morgan until neither of us could move.

And pray no more visions came to haunt me of impending doom, hers or anyone else's.

"Last box," Dagon announced, walking through the front door.

"Cheers to that," Zane said, clinking his beer against Mack's. "Can one of you please explain to us again why you're renting a house in, what town are we in again?"

"Oak Hollow," I said. "And we're helping out Dagon's brother for a while. I'm taking some time away, and Dagon is, too. We have some stuff we want to figure out while not worrying about classes. And we're not that far away from you guys."

Dagon came to stand beside me, kissing the top of my head. It'd been hard to be apart from each other for more than a few minutes after what went down with Kayla. Not that I was complaining. I quite enjoyed having Dagon attached at the hip right now. It'd be even better once Mack and Zane headed out. We'd have our new cottage all to ourselves. I had a few ideas on how to celebrate moving in together. Dagon's hand tightened on my hip, and I winked up at him.

Thankfully, we didn't have to see anyone else until tomorrow. Jasmine had invited us over for dinner and to hang out then. Our new jobs didn't start until the following week. Dagon would be working with Calrod and Arkon as another handyman, and Jasmine had offered me a job at her antique store. Between that and taking up the position to help Cyrene and work at the Witch Archives, I'd be busy enough. And both jobs kept me close to Dagon. Right now, that was all I wanted. We might've stopped Kayla, but the bounty hunters working for Prince Carridan could always come back. And who was to say another crazy psycho like Kayla wouldn't pop up? Besides, staying in Oak Hollow gave Dagon a chance to be himself more often. It'd be good for both of us to take a break and be around family.

My new family.

I wasn't able to stop smiling the rest of the afternoon while Mack and Zane helped us unpack. By the time they left that evening, I was anxious to share with Dagon what I'd purchased specially for tonight. I'd been careful all day not to think about it. Once the front door was locked, and we were alone, I darted to the bedroom with him right behind me.

"What are you up to?" he asked, leaning against the doorframe.

"Nothing."

"Liar," he whispered huskily, his gaze raking over me in my baggy t-shirt and tight jeans. He licked his lips and took a step into the room, but I shook my head.

"Not yet. Got you a present."

I shooed him out of the doorway. Just as the door was closing, Dagon snarled. He was on his knees when I threw the door back open. His claws dug into the hardwood floor and his back arched. His body curled in on itself, and he growled, gnashing his teeth. His body was burning up when I laid my hand on his shoulder to steady him. Words came out of his mouth, but they were demonic. He yelled like he was in pain and fell into me, shaking.

"He's coming," he whispered. His head shot up, and he gripped my arms. "He's coming."

"Who? Dagon? Look at me," I said when his gaze

darted wildly around. Was he still trapped in the vision? "What did you see? Who's coming?"

"Carridan," Dagon said, and my heart stuttered. "Prince Carridan is coming to Oak Hollow."

AFTERWORD

Click for more Ava Benton works!

Sign up for the newsletter to be notified of new releases.

Click on link for

Newsletter

or put this in your browser window:

mailerlite.com/webforms/landing/m7a8c5